Masked

....

Dianna Berryman

Contents

Chapter 1

From the Redwood Police Department office desk, forty-five-year-old Homicide Detective Robert Maxwell, was looking through photographs of victims from the table. Despair was on his face when he stared at the images of ten men and women that were horribly disfigured. Humidity stifled the air. Robert's face was sweaty. He even ignored the divorce papers laying at his desk that was severed to him today, dreading the mistake that cost him his marriage. It was hard for Robert to shake the reality of his situation.

In the span of his twenty five year career, he never saw anything like these murders. Robert rubbed his light brown forehead in frustration, his fingers curved against his short black Caesar haircut. The killings were ritualistic and they followed a particular pattern. He sat and thought for a moment. Looking at the pictures, Robert noticed a letter "a" carved into the victims head. The arms and legs were severed from the victims body and some missing their eyes or tongues. He felt the killings were done by a copycat that mimicked the Scavenger of Redwood, Washington. This killer was notorious for his heinous crimes, evading capture for the past decade. But it didn't explain the recent murders that had been piling up in the county under the radar and Robert didn't believe in coincidence.

Detective Maxwell heard a knock at the door. "Come in."

An officer opened the door and walked in. "You got a visitor."

"Okay, send them in," Robert replied, placing the images back into a folder along with the divorce papers, while closing it up, and concealing it in his desk drawer.

He adjusted the red tie around the collar of his neck. A young woman came into his office. It was someone he recognized. It was Jennifer Myers, his son Jordan's girlfriend, whom he hadn't seen in two years. She was wearing a brown coat that covered her Diner outfit. Her brown hair wrapped in a bun, her brown eyes spoke of fear and worry. She sat herself down on a brown chair. This was the first time Jennifer entered Robert's office. Her awkward glance at him was clear.

"Jennifer, what brings you here?" Robert asked. "It has been a while since I last saw you. How's that grandson of mine Kevin?"

"He is getting bigger," Jennifer smiled. She showed a picture of Kevin from her cell phone to Robert.

"Kevin asked about you." Jennifer smiled.

Robert smirked, taking her cell phone to look at the picture. "Handsome little devil. He got my nose. How is Jordan?"

"Yeah, Kevin is," Jennifer gasped for a moment. "There is something I need to talk to you about."

"Okay," Robert replied.

"It's about Jordan, he is missing."

He lost eye contact with Jennifer as the information of what she said flooded in, while placing her cell phone on the table. Robert's heart began to pound faster as panic filled his eyes, knowing his son was missing. Fear and dread overwhelmed his senses. The idea that a maniac kidnapped his son put him on edge.

"Missing, what do you mean?" Robert inquired, handing back her cell phone

"He hasn't returned my calls. He has been gone for days. It is not like him to do that and he always texts and calls me. I am really worried. Kevin cried, missing his Dad. It is hard for both of us."

"Can you tell me when was the last time you saw Jordan?"

"Okay, Jordan and I were invited to our neighbor Mark Field's birthday."

"Where is his address?"

"Sunnyside Ave on 9 Street."

"I'm gonna find him," Robert reached for his black coat from the chair, while walking out with Jennifer from the office, opening the door for her to exit the room. "I will need you and Kevin to stay over at Amber's. You think you can do that?"

"Yeah, I can," Jennifer gave a reassuring look.

"Alright," Robert walked to the door.

"Where are you going?" she asked.

He turned and said," To do what I do best."

One officer called out to him from the hallway. "Detective Maxwell, there was a murder at 8 Pond Ave. A triple homicide."

"Get Ross on the case," Robert said in a stern tone, walking out of the police department.

Robert walked toward his car. He heard a beeping noise from his cell phone when he reached for his pocket. His eyes lit up at what he saw. Robert's head was spinning. It was a picture of Jordan bound by rope on the table with a white gag over his mouth. At the back of the photo, was a phone number to call. He quickly called the number and it rang two times. Someone picked up on the other end.

"Hello, Detective Maxwell. It is so good to hear your voice. I hope you enjoy the present I sent you," the Masked killer said.

"Where is my son you sick fuck?" Robert demanded.

"Wow, Detective, I didn't know I would get a rise out of you so soon," the masked killer said, chuckling with a disturbing laughter. "Your son is alive for now."

"Put him on the phone," Robert demanded.

"No, he can't come to the phone now," the masked killer said.

"I will find you, Robert gripped the phone,"When I do, I'll put a bullet in your head."

"I would like to see you try. But first, I want you to play a game for me. Think of it as "hide and seek." I just texted you an address where I want you to go. There you will find a clue. If I don't hear from you in the next hour, I will be mailing pieces of your son to you the next business day. We will keep in touch, Detective Maxwell!" The Masked killer hung up the phone.

Robert was beside himself, banging his hand on the steering wheel, cursing up a storm. If he didn't play the killer's game, he would lose his son. Jennifer would never forgive him and his grandson would be fatherless. He had to act fast. Time was running out for Jordan. He couldn't fail his son and he would do what was necessary to save him.

"I will find you Jordan," Robert said, promising himself. "I will get you back to Jennifer. I won't fail you son."

* * *

Darkness surrounded the room. Jordan Maxwell woke up hands and ankles bound by rope on the wooden table as if ready for a sacrifice. He yelled for help. Fear echoed in his rasped voice. How he regretted going out to a neighbor's birthday party and ended up in a place like this.The lights came on. Jordan noticed plastic covering the floor and walls. Baby doll heads painted in white, hanging from the ceiling on wire. There were many disturbing photographic images plastered on the wall. They depicted images of mutilated bodies. Jordan almost vomited. What creeped him out the most, was that the victims from the photographs were missing eyes and had deep cravings of a letter on their heads.

Jordan heard heavy footsteps, coming down the steps. He lifted his head and saw a man dressed in blue Jeans, black sweater, with a black hood. He had a golden mask on his face that showed no expression. In his hand, he held a big kitchen knife with a brown hilt. The blade glistened against the light.

"Please, don't kill me," Jordan pleaded. "I have a girlfriend and a baby boy. You can take my money and call it a day."

The Masked killer walked up, observing him. He watched him breathe heavily as he placed the blade against his throat. Jordan didn't say a word, sensing if he uttered a word, he would die.

"I don't want your money," the Masked killer said in a mechanical voice. "My needs are much more in-depth," The Masked killer said, teasing Jordan's right face with the blade.

"Please, I have a family," Jordan said, trying to plead with him. The masked killer put pressure on Jordan's throat with glaring cold eyes.

"Say one more word. One more word that comes out of your mouth, will be your last," the Masked killer said.

Jordan remained silent. He heard a shaky man's voice and bangs from the other room. The Masked killer took the knife off of Jordan's throat. He walked away to open a brown wooden door to the other room. The Masked killer closed the door behind himself. Jordan gasped for a moment. He struggled to break free from his confines. Jordan grunted in frustration. He heard something familiar. It was his cell phone ringing by the table next to him. He knew his girl-friend, Jennifer, was calling him. Jordan strained, reaching the table with his right foot. It was three inches from the table. Jordan swung his right foot, hitting against the table with his shoe.

The cell phone fell on the floor. He cursed under his breath. The man in the other room screamed louder with a cry. It sounded as if an animal was put to death. Jordan heard silence from the man in the other room. There were several loud thuds that sounded off with squishing noises. It made him nervous and started to freak him out.

Sweat was forming on his face as he squirmed to break free of his restraints.

Jordan heard something close to him as he wiggled against the rope. He looked over to his left, Jordan saw someone come out of a crawl space. It was a boy about ten years of age that had pale skin. He was dressed in tattered dark clothes and had brown shoes with holes in them. The boy walked over to Jordan out of the shadows. Eager to meet the captive in an enthusiastic manner.

"Hey, what is your name?" Jordan asked in a level tone.

"My name is Sam," the boy said with curious eyes.

Nice to meet you, Sam. Can you do me a favor? I'm a bit tied up. Can you get me my cell phone for me," Jordan said pointing to the cellphone that was two inches from his foot.

Sam stared at Jordan. He picked up the cell phone like it was foreign to him. "Okay." He walked slowly to Jordan with the phone in hand and was about to hand it to him.

Then, out of the blue, Sam heard footsteps from the wooden panel above him. "I am not supposed to be here." Out of fear, he dropped the cell phone on the corner of the table and went back into the crawl space.

"Wait, I need my cell phone," Jordan whispered.

Without hesitation, Jordan, with all his strength, kicked his cell phone under the table. He took a moment to breathe. Fearful of what's to come. The door opened. The Masked killer walked in with blood, covering his sweater and pants. Droplets of blood leaked from his hands. Hope was fleeting for Jordan. His only move was to keep the cell phone out of the Masked killer's sight. Jordan had to swallow his pride. He only thought of one simple intention, calling his father. But could he keep the Masked killer busy enough to do it? All Jordan had to do was stay alive long enough to do just that.

"Now, we are going to have some fun," the Masked killer said. "Just you wait and see. I don't get to kill you tonight."

"So, does that mean you will let me go?" Jordan inquired.

"Why would I do a thing like that? I can't have you running around to the police," the Masked killer said. "I have other plans for you."

Chapter 2

Robert parked his red 2019 Jaguar hybrid car at the parking spot that was vacant. He stared from the window, eyeing a yellow complex home in contempt. No lights were visible. His heart was pounding fast, grabbing his gun off the seat. He counted to five to calm himself. Robert couldn't allow his emotions to distract him when it came to saving his son. He had to be ready for the unexpected. Even from the Masked killer. Robert got out from the car, feeling the cool breeze against his body. He treaded on the damp grass up the hill, looking side to side pointing his gun. His eyes narrowed at the complex. Without hesitation, Robert pulled out his cell phone and dialed a number.

"I'm here." Robert walked on the grass, pointing his forward.

"Good, come inside. I have so much to show you, so much to explore." The Masked killer made a chilling laugh.

Robert ended the call and approached the door, feeling the knob with his hand with caution. He turned the knob unlocking the door. Robert flipped the white switch on the corner of the wall. He walked slowly as he passed the paintings of the white walls. He noticed the abstract art of trees, birds, and a couple of people, holding hands on the corner of his eye. Robert walked toward the living room with his gun. In front of him were three barrels with red X marks on them. There was a timer on one of them. "What do you value the most, Detective Maxwell? Tell me is it the thrill of the hunt? Capturing criminals? No, no there is something more."

"Why don't you come out and find out?" Robert asked, pointing his gun to the corner.

"Now we are going to play a fun game. All you have to do is solve my riddle and select the right barrel to find a clue. If not, the barrels will explode, releasing a neurotoxin gas that would disrupt your nervous system, causing permanent nerve damage, blindness, memory loss, and my particular favorite death. Are you ready to play? Here is my riddle. I am balanced and never off my game when everything else fails, what am I? You have two minutes to solve my riddle. I suggest you choose the correct answer."

Robert put his gun away and looked at the barrels, trying to decide which one to open. He thought long and hard about the riddle, deciphering its meaning. Robert closed his eyes, canceling out the noise from his head of the timer. He took a deep breath and paused. "I am balanced and never off my game when everything else fails?" Robert asked himself. Robert paced back and forth. "Of course, I am centered. That has to be the answer."

Just under fifty-eight seconds, Robert opened the lid at the center barrel and said his last prayers under his breath. The timer had stopped. Robert reached inside, finding a piece of paper and golden key. "Well done! But the game is far from over and there are more games to play."

Robert yelled at the top of his lungs. "I did what you wanted. I want my son!"

"If you don't play the rest of the game, he dies. It's that simple. The question is how far are you willing to go to save your son Jordan? I have no problem slitting his throat and chopping him into little pieces."

Robert frowned, gripping his right hand. He wanted nothing more than to find the killer and kill him with his bare hands, watching the life drain from his eyes. Jordan was all he had and he couldn't afford to lose him. More than ever, Robert was determined and nothing was gonna get in his way. Even if it meant searching the whole neighborhood rain or shine.

"Now, open the white door at the corner."

Robert drew out his weapon again as he opened the door. He leaned in, pointing his gun side to side as he walked inside the dark room. As Robert walked further up, he slipped against a severed hand that displayed a trail of blood, which led into a straight line. On the side of him, he noticed a severed head with no eyes with a deep craving of a letter A on its head. Panic overcame him. A shrill scream escaped Robert's mouth. He took a deep breath, trying to clear his head at what he saw. Robert felt relief that he wasn't under attack. He got up from the blood covered floor and continued to walk.

Robert followed a trail of blood into a room. A light came on in the room. He saw a man with brown eyes, a white polo shirt, and blue Jean's trapped inside a glass case. The man banged at the glass in desperation. "Get me out of here!"

"Larry White, son of late Officer Corey White, is here to pay for his sins. Open the note, Detective." Robert unraveled the note from his hand that read, "Set Him Free."

"What is the meaning of this note?" Robert asked.

"Use the key to set him free and he will live."

Robert was skeptical of his words. He slowly placed the golden key into the keyhole slot. Robert turned the key counter-clockwise. The door opened in the room. Corey smiled for a moment, but it ended when he stepped back with his feet against a wire. A shotgun fired from behind at him, hitting his lower back. As he plummeted to the floor in agony, a mechanical axe came down like a guillotine from the ceiling, and severed his head in a swift motion. Blood splattered across the glass.

"You said to set him free. I did what you ask! Why did you kill him?"

The Masked killer laughed. "You set him free alright and you did so well. What do you think it would be that easy this time? My work is not done. I wish I could stay and chat, but I got other people to pay a visit too. Will keep in touch."

"I want my son back. I will find you. Do you hear me? If anything happens to my son, I will fucking kill you!" Robert pushed items off the table, clenching his teeth.

"Later, Detective Maxwell."

Hours later the police arrived at the yellow complex. With their cars giving off red and blue flashes of light. Many police blocked other tenants from entering the area with yellow caution tape and brown barricades. News Reporters and camera crew were hovering the area like vultures, trying to get the inside scoop of the murders.

Chief of Police, Katie Campbell, was there at the scene, wearing her conservative grey suit, button black blouse, and dark horn rim glasses with black curly hair. Her arrival caused Robert uneasiness and tension within him with the questioning of the events that happened. The fact that his son was still missing ate at his soul. He never imagined Jordan would be kidnapped by a demented serial killer. A dangerous one who evaded capture.

"So, that's your story Robert?" Katie asked to confirm everything.

"That is my story." Robert crossed his arms.

"What do you know so far about our suspect?" Katie asked.

"This guy is a fanatic killer driven by a need to punish and likes to play games. Wait! There is something else. The victim was Corey White. I knew his father twenty-five years ago."

"So, you are saying a serial killer is targeting officers that once served our department. There has to be a connection."

"Yes, Captain, that is actually what I'm saying. For some reason, the killer is obsessed with me. He has my son... I need you to send the police over to protect Jennifer and my grandson. Maybe move them into a safe house for protection."

"Consider it done. You should go home Robert. We got it from here." Katie held on to his shoulder. "Take a day to yourself."

"I can't do that. I need to find him and stop him." Robert pulled away. "I won't rest until I find my son. The sick bastard told me his work is not done, which means he is gonna kill again soon."

"Go home, Robert." Katie stared up at him. "That is an order. I expect to have a full paperwork by my desk on Monday."

Robert walked away. "Oh, you know how I feel about paperwork. As for going home, that is not an option."

* * *

Jordan checked around to see if anyone was around the room. It was quiet. He laid on the table still bound, looking at the walls with the doll heads on wires. The eerie emptiness of their eyes sent chills to Jordan's spine. He felt as if closed off from civilization that suffocated him.

Jordan made sure the Masked killer left the perimeter to make his move. He reached for his cell phone in silence and realized the battery on his phone was at 1% and the phone went dead. Jordan cursed under his tongue. He heard a noise and hid his cell phone in his pocket and remained still. Something moved in the shadows. Then, it came closer to Jordan's direction as a hand reached out to his shoulder. Jordan jerked back in shock, eyes bulged when he saw it was Sam.

"Oh, you scared the daylights out of me."

"I'm sorry, I didn't mean to scare you."

"It's okay Sam, I had a rough night. I am just a little hungry and thirsty."

"Oh, I can get you some food and something to drink but it will be our little secret."

"I can keep a secret and I won't tell anyone."

"I will be right back."

Sam went back into the crawl space and was gone for thirty minutes. Jordan's stomach growled at him like a lion. He waited and waited for Sam's return. Jordan heard footsteps. He lifted his head and saw it was Sam with a brown bag of food and water. "I got you a sandwich and water. I hope you like it."

Jordan smirked."Like it, Sam? I will eat anything."

Sam opened a bag and gave Jordan a half chicken sandwich with lettuce and sliced tomatoes. Since Jordan's tied up, Sam put the sandwich in his mouth to chew and gave him some water.

"Oh, that hit the spot. Thank you, Sam, you are a good boy."

"Does that mean we are friends?"

Jordan beamed with a smile. "Yes, we are friends."

Sam's face lit up with a smile. "You're my first friend here. Don't worry, I won't let him hurt you. We are gonna be the best of friends." Sam hugged Jordan.

The doorknob started to turn from the door. Sam heard noise and stood up. Jordan looked at the door. The door opened and the masked killer entered, glaring at the boy with his brown angry eyes.

"What are you doing here?" The Masked killer asked.

"He is my new friend. I won't let you hurt him." Sam stood in front of him.

"Go to your room Sam," the masked killer placed his bloody gloved hand at the door.

"No, I won't let you hurt Jordan." Sam stood back.

The masked killer's hand tightened at the door. "I won't ask again to leave now or get a whipping."

Sam turned and looked at Jordan. "I will be back, my friend. I promise."Sam left through the front door and the Masked killer closed it.

"Now it is just the two of us. I have to say your father put up a show tonight."

"How do you know my father?" Jordan asked.

"Let's just say I have watched your father for some time. I have followed his every move." The Masked killer went over to the side to pull up his cell phone, recording Jordan on the table.

"What are you doing?" Jordan asked.

The Masked killer pulled out his small knife from his coat and twirled it around professionally. He threw the knife against the wall, missing Jordan's head. The Masked killer pulled out his big knife from a table and placed it against his throat.

"You are asking so many questions." The blade nicked a part of Jordan's neck. "I should kill you now and deliver what's part of you to your father. I could start with your fingers. How about I pick out these eyes of yours and deliver them to your dear father? No, that wouldn't work right away. I have other plans for you." The Masked killer placed a white gag over his mouth.

"Now that is better," the Masked killer brought out a black tool box from under the table. He placed the box on the table next to Jordan, opened it up, touching the blades with his fingers, as if it was calling out to him to select the perfect one.

Jordan struggled against the ropes, mumbling in protest. "There, there it won't hurt one bit. Just wait and see."

Chapter 3

It was past midnight and Robert couldn't rest after driving across the neighborhood, searching for any clues that would lead to finding Jordan. Each search led to one dead end after the other. Robert drove down toward the Royal Eights bar off on Route 85, which was about five miles from his home. The lights illuminated inside the bar, giving off a glow, which mirrored the people inside with their laughter and whispers. His mind faded away from the mindless chatter of a drunk man, making advances to women with a one-liner. He gave them dirty looks while drinking more.

The Royal Eight bar had a long history. Since it was owned by the Ross family for twenty years, Robert's police cadet and friend, Nathan Ross, would always invite him with the guys to let loose and eat barbecue chicken wings or pretzels. Of course, Robert was in denial, thinking being at the bar would help him cope with the massacre he witnessed at the housing complex. How he bit his lower lip whenever he had a flashback of Larry White's brutal murder, or when the blood at the scene soiled his clothes. Along with a decapitated head, which had no eyes and a severed hand. His eyes would close, drinking down more alcohol. He took his time swallowing it, feeling the sweet-bitter taste. How it burned his throat, how he relished it.

Robert took his cell phone out of his pocket and stared at the photo he took of Jordan. Lack of sleep and booze didn't help. Robert brows furrowed deep. His head was pounding like a drum nonstop. Veins developed around his temple. He pounded the table twice. He couldn't contain the rage that was building up like a volcano inside of his heart. The people around him were disturbed by Robert's outburst. A beautiful blonde waitress who wore dark Jeans and a t-shirt. She had blue eyes that approached his soul.

"Sir, are you alright?" The waitress looked at him.

Robert came back to his senses and rubbed his eyes. "Yeah, I am okay."

"You don't look okay. Do you want to talk about it?" The waitress asked.

"Not right now. What is your name?"

"My name is Barbara."

"A pleasure to meet you, Barbara. My name is Robert."

"Hey, I want my pretzels," one guy shouted.

"I'm sorry. I have to get back to work," Barbara said.

"I understand duty calls," Robert said.

Robert watched Barbara walk away. But reality hit him, knowing that his son was still missing. Apart from himself felt guilty for being distracted. He eyed the bartender and waved his hand. "Hey, the bartender, can I get another hit?"

"What can I get you?"The bartender asked.

Robert replied. "Give me another shot of that Jack Daniel's from the top shelf. Hey, what happened to Nathan? I haven't seen him in a while."

The bartender smiled. Oh, Nathan, yeah he is on vacation. He should be back next week. "Your drink is coming right up."

"Thanks."

The bartender looked into Robert's distorted face with a frown. "Is everything alright?"

Robert looked at him with his blurry vision. "I had better days." He gulped down another drink. He pushed the shot glass forward. "Hit me again."

Robert's breath reeked heavily of booze. His liver didn't thank him for each shot of alcohol he consumed. He lost count of how many drinks he had. The floors within the bar were pristine with cherry oak wood. The bar table consisted of black marble.

The barstool Robert sat on was composed of metal chrome with black rubber comfort patting. On the far corner, one multicolored Junk Box of red, blue, and yellow located in the far back played loud music. People in that area played pool and danced like there was no tomorrow.

The smell of smoke left an everlasting scent in the air. The music seemed to blur in the background. Nothing mattered at the moment for Robert since his shot glass was empty as the void in his heart after. Robert tapped his fingers on the marble table.

One man tapped his shoulder and replied. "Aren't you gonna buy me a drink?"

Robert turned around and saw it was Kenny Rogers, an ex-cop and former marine. Having a bald head with brown eyes, wearing a black shirt and blue Jeans. On the right of him, were retired cops Aran Boon, Justin Henderson, and Gabriel Logan.

"It has been a long time, fellas," Robert said.

Robert stood up from the stool and greeted them with smiles and hugs. The men had a seat. "What brings you all here?"

Robert got the attention of the bartender. "Hey, my friends here would like some drinks."

"Okay, what can I get you?" The bartender asked, eyeing the group.

"Just regular beer," Kenny said. "The same for the rest of the group. We heard what happened to Larry. The funeral was going to be on Wednesday."

"Larry did not deserve that he was like a son to me," Gabriel said, banging his head on the table.

The people from the bar took notice and then minded their own business. "I know the feeling. I remember going fishing with him and his father," Justin said. Justin's tone shifted. "Honestly, I would like to catch the fucker who did this."

"I agree with you on that," Robert said, downing another shot of Jack Daniel's and eating pretzels on a tray.

"Hey, you never told me about Jordan. How is he?" Kenny asked.

Robert looked at Kenny with a deadpan look. "My son has been kidnapped. I failed him, Kenny, I failed him."

Kenny touched Robert's shoulder."Hey, Robert, we got your back. Anything you need."

"I need your help to find my boy," Robert said.

"You know I'm down for that," Gabriel said.

"What do you say, Justin, are you in?" Robert asked.

They all looked at Justin as he raised his beer bottle at the group. "I'm all the way in."

Robert left a tip at the marble table."Okay, let's get out of here." Robert stumbled. Kenny caught him. "I got yeah Robert."

The bartender observed what happened and collected the tip from the table. He noticed it was a twenty-dollar tip. The bartender sneaked the twenty in his pocket like he won a lottery ticket. A smile spread across his face when he watched as the men left the bar.

Kenny suggested. "Hey, you can roll with me. You can leave your car here and in the morning we can come back here to pick it up. We wouldn't want our detective pulled over for a DWI."

"Yeah, I guess you are right," Robert said.

Kenny smiled. "Of course I am right. Say how is Captain Cambell? Is she still busting your balls?"

"Yeah, she still is the same," Robert explained. "She had the nerve to send me home when the killer was still out there. No, I won't rest until I find my son."

"Don't worry, Robert, we will help you find this scumbag. You have my word on that," Kenny said. "Did you get a good look at him?"

"No, I never did. He called me through my cell phone," Robert said. "The guy never showed his face."

"Hey, Gabriel, your nephew is good with computers, right? Do you think he could run a trace on his phone?" Kenny asked.

"I can't see why not. I'll give him a call," Gabriel said as he reached for his phone."

"I think it would be better if we come up with a plan," Robert said.

"I agree. How about we all meet at the Cabins at Say Shore," Kenny suggested to the group. The group all agreed. "Okay, then it is settled, we will all be there by 12 pm."

It was morning. Robert got up from the bed. He felt his hangover the next day. He walked over to the bathroom to do his business and clean himself up. Robert walked out of the bathroom and smelled bacon in the air. He put on his shoes and headed downstairs. As Robert walked further up from the hall, straight ahead into the kitchen, he noticed Kenny making pancakes and flipping eggs with a spatula with skill.

"Good Morning!" Kenny said.

"Ah, Good Morning," Robert said sitting by the table. He reached for his cell phone to take it off the charger.

"I made some coffee. The creamer is on your side if you need it."

"Thanks, I appreciate it."

Robert's cell phone started to ring. He saw it was his ex-wife Amber calling. "I will be right back Kenny, it's Amber."

"Okay, tell her I said Hello."

"I will," Robert said, getting up from the chair and heading to the living room. He answered.

"Hello Amber, how is everything?"

"Hello, Detective Maxwell!"

Robert gasped at the voice of the Masked killer. "What do you want?"

"I want to have a nice chat with you. Aren't you gonna ask me how your son is? I have to say your boy is quite the screamer. Did he get that from you, or from your former wife? Oh, sweet Amber, how she sleeps in her queen-size bed in that pretty white house. She is quite the looker. Easy on the eyes." The masked killer sent photos of Amber in her bed sleeping. Then, she sent photos of her white house.

"You leave her alone. This is between you and me."

"What's the matter, Detective Maxwell, did I hit a nerve? How does it feel to lose people close to you? Do you feel helpless? How do you sleep at night knowing I have your boy all to myself? So many tools I can use to carve that pretty face of his and the same with his mother. I didn't know your wife was a moaner. It kind of turned me on. I can see why you picked her. How I would love to collect her head and her pretty delicate hands."

"Listen here whoever you are... I'm coming for you and I will kill you."

"Oh, that's what I want, Detective Maxwell. I'm looking forward to our game. "I left a little surprise at Amber's house. A nice package at her front step. See you soon, Detective Maxwell." The masked killer hangs up.

"Shit!"

Robert walked back toward the kitchen. "Kenny, I need your keys and your spare gun."

"What's going on?"

"It's Amber, I think she is trouble."

"I am coming with you. I will send the text to let the guys meet us there," Kenny said, turning off the stove and grabbing his keys and two guns. He hands one gun over to Robert.

Robert and Kenny left the Cabin of Say Shore and were on the road. Kenny was driving as fast as he could on the main thruway. He turned on his signal and turned right on the road. He took Exit 15 on the ramp and sped through the road.

In less than forty-five minutes, they arrived at Amber's house and Kenny parked his car on the sidewalk. He turned off the engine. They both got out of the car with their guns out. Robert walked five blocks. He signaled Kenny to follow, waving his hand. Robert went up to the steps and below he found a box wrapped in a blue shiny gift wrap. He knocked on the door with a firm hand. He knocked on the door again. "Amber!" Robert yelled and there was no response. Robert kicked the door open, pointing his gun. Kenny followed behind him.

"I will check the living room," Kenny whispered to Robert.

"Amber!" Robert yelled going up the stairs.

Robert walked up the stairs. Avoiding the staircase railings, he made it to the top. Robert leaned against the wall and peaced up the steps as he checked the hallway to make sure it was clear. He approached a white door. Robert took a step back and kicked the door down. When he walked into the room, his face contorted when

he found a photo of Amber on her bed tied and gagged. He turned
the photo over to a message that read "I have her too!"

Chapter 4

Kenny ran up the stairs to check on Robert. He held his hand on the staircase railings. Kenny reached the top floor. His face perspired with sweat and he started to breathe hard. The silence made him uneasy as he walked the hallway. There was a sense of uncertainty. He walked slowly. Just to avoid the creaking noise of the hardwood floor.

Kenny went into the room with his gun out. He saw Robert on his knees by the bed. "Robert, are you okay?" He let his gun down and went up to him and touched his shoulder.

Kenny noticed Robert's frown on his face and scrunched up lips. Then, his eyes picked up on the photo of Amber on the bed. "Oh, my God!"

Robert said no words. No amount of words could comfort him at this moment. Kenny's voice echoed at the back of his mind, ignoring what he was saying. Blood rushed to his brain. Robert's hands tightened, his palm and fingers formed into a tight ball, waiting to hit something. He got up from the floor and walked out of the room. He went downstairs toward the front door.

At the corner of his eye, he saw the blue gift-wrapped package on the step. Without even thinking about it, Robert picked up the gift-wrapped box, ripped off the blue wrapping and opened a white box. Robert gasped at what he saw. It was a severed hand that had a gold class ring. There was a green ruby gem embedded at the center with a gold band inscription "Law Enforcement" attached to the index finger. What was special about that ring was the fact that it belonged to someone from the police academy. It was the kind of ring given to policemen before they get their certificate and police badge after graduation. But who did this hand belong to? These were questions Robert wrestled with from the depths of his mind.

"This is not a coincidence." Something caught Robert's attention when he turned the handover, exposing an inner palm. Inside the palm was a message that read "RJ," which made Robert's spine cringe. Yet, he felt the message had meaning. It had some type of connection. A clue to the past of the killer he thought. The name RJ was familiar. He knew that name came from a serial killer known as the "Chameleon." A serial killer that he and a former partner had dealt with in the past. Could it be him? He wondered.

Kenny was still in Amber's room, looking for more clues. He stumbled upon the closet that was close to him. When Kenny opened the door, the Masked killer lunged into him with a sharp blade and stabbed him repeatedly in the stomach. He winced in pain, falling on his back, dropping the gun.

The Masked killer got on top of Kenny and took the bloody blade out of his stomach and tried to stab him in the chest with it. With quick reflexes, Kenny grabbed hold of the Masked killer's wrist, while he struggled to reach for the gun with his other hand. His hand was inches away from the gun.

"Why don't you die like a good boy! I would love to carve out your eyes." The Masked killer pressed on Kenny's wound on his stomach. "Ahh!" Kenny screamed and grabbed hold of his gun. He opened fire at the Masked killer's shoulder, causing him to flinch back. Before another shot was fired, the Masked killer dodged the two other bullets with forwarding rolls and jumped through the window. He landed two stories in the backyard like a cat and he climbed up the wooden fence, dropping down into the grass. The Masked killer got in his dark-tinted van and drove off.

Robert heard the commotion and ran back inside the house toward Amber's room. He felt air coming out through the shattered window. As he walked closer, he found Kenny, bleeding out on the floor. He went to him and held him up. Robert called 911 on his cell phone.

Kenny was bleeding through his mouth. "I got him." Robert ripped a piece of cloth and wrapped around Kenny's wound to stop the bleeding.

"The bastard was quick, I saw him. He had a gold mask. Blue pants, black sweater with a hoodie. His height had to be 6' 1." Promise me one thing, Robert! Don't let this son of a bitch roam free. He is pure evil."

"Hello 911! What's your emergency?"

"Yes, my friend has been stabbed! Please hurry..."

"Is he still conscious? Where has he been stabbed?"

"Yes, he is still conscious. He has been stabbed in the stomach. The address is 122 North Walnut Avenue. House number 25. Did you get that?"

"Yes, I got it. We are sending someone down," the operator said.

"Thank you!"Robert said, hanging up the cell phone. "I'm here Kenny, the ambulance is coming."

Police and ambulance sirens were heard outside. Flashing blue and red lights shined through the opening. A cool breeze blew in their direction. "They are here Kenny I told you they would come--" When Robert looked at Kenny's face, he realized Kenny lost consciousness.

Two hours had passed, Robert was at the hospital waiting room with his other friends Gabriel, Aran, and Justin. They each stared at each other in momentary silence. Nobody pictured Kenny would be in a hospital of all places with multiple stab wounds in the gut. The man survived the war in the front lines as a US Marine and as a police officer.

"Okay, I will say it. Kenny didn't deserve this. Whoever did this is going down," Robert said. "I mean for peeks sake. The psycho kidnapped Amber. We need to get more police officers involved. This guy won't escape justice."

"I agree with you one hundred percent, Aran said. "I know Kenny will pull through. He's tough as they come."

"I'm going to get some air," Justin said. He got up from the chair and walked out of the room.

"I will be back, nature calls," Gabriel said.

Robert got a call. It was from Captain Kate Cambell. "Hello."

"Robert, I thought I told you to go home. Not to drag this publicity stunt."

"The killer has Amber and my son."

"You should have informed me about yourself instead of doing things on your own. Now, the FBI has taken over this case."

"The killer is still out there. He is trying to send me a message. He put Kenny in a freaking hospital."

"My hands are tied. You leave me no choice."

"What are you trying to say, Captain?"

"I'm taking you off the force. You are suspended until further notice. I want your badge and gun by the end of tonight." She hung up on Robert.

"Well, my night gets more interesting," Robert said. "Captain Cambell suspended me. The FBI is running the show."

"That sucks. Sorry to hear that," Aran said.

"It doesn't matter. I needed a vacation from the force. Besides, I still have a killer to track down."

A doctor came into the waiting room dressed in a white coat. He had glasses and grey hair. He expressed a smile on his face.

"Hello, I'm Doctor Lacroix. I have some good news Kenny will pull through. We managed to patch up his stomach. He will need to be in the hospital for four days. Just for observation."

"That's good to hear, Doc. Can we see him?" Robert asked.

"Sure you can follow me," Doctor Lacroix said.

Robert and Aran followed Doctor Lacroix. They passed through the halls congested by nurses and other medical staff until approaching room 19. Aran texted Gabriel and Justin that Kenny is okay to find us in room 19.

Robert saw Kenny connected to tubes and IV's. He was lying in bed wrapped in a blanket, watching FBI Most Wanted. "Hey, stranger!"

"Hey, you guys thank you for coming," Kenny said with a warm smile.

"How are you feeling?" Aran asked.

"Oh, I feel good. The nurse gave me some powerful painkillers. Where are the others?" Kenny asked.

"They should be on their way," Robert said.

Kenny adjusted his pillow. "I am really glad you guys came."

"Hey, a friend in need is a friend indeed," Aran said with a wink. "Hey, did you know that Robert got suspended. Now, the FBI has taken over jurisdiction since that serial killer is making a name for himself. That is the thing about serial killers, they are all narcissistic in nature. They feel a sense of self-importance."

"That doesn't matter," Robert said. I want to find my family. Do you remember anything specific about the killer?"

Kenny looked closely at Robert about to deliver on the chilling details of his resilience,"The one thing I do recall was his voice. It sounded like one of these mechanical voices you hear in horror movies. Besides that and the golden mask. I remember seeing his eyes. They were brown."

"Thank you, Kenny, that will do," Robert said.

Robert had received a text message from his phone. He decides to open up the message. He noticed a video message, showing an image of Amber on a cold table unconscious and bound by black rope. Robert pressed the play button on his phone. "Hello, Detective Maxwell, did you get my gift? I hope I didn't ruin your day. As you know, I have your wife and son." The Masked killer touches her hair with dark gloves. "I have to say your wife has soft skin. She would make a good collection for my work. Oh, those soft lips. You have good taste, Detective. I want you to meet me at this address and this time I want you to come alone. No cops. Just you and me. If you don't meet my terms, well, you will see parts of Jordan and Amber each week at your front doorstep. You have three hours to decide. I hope to hear from you soon." The video message ended on Robert's cell phone.

"Please don't tell me you are going to play along with his games," Kenny said with a frown.

Robert shrugged his shoulders and sighed. "I have no choice. He has them. I need to do this alone."

"That's suicide man you know that. Let us help," Aran said.

"He said no cops," Robert stated.

"Let's time I check, we are retired cops," Aran replied.

"Or you could let Captain Cambell know what's going on," Kenny said.

"It's bad enough she suspended me already. I don't think Captain Cambell will hear me out."

"Doesn't hurt to try and besides we got your back," Kenny said.

"Hey, Gabriel and Justin haven't shown up. I wonder what these two are up to?" Kenny said.

"Hey, I will be right back. I'm gonna get some coffee," Robert said. "Do you want anything Aran?"

"Not really. "Yeah, go ahead. I will keep an eye out on Kenny here," Aran said.

Robert left room 19. He walked the halls, passing by nurses. He noticed one custodian, mopping near the cafeteria. "Hey, do you know where I can get some coffee?"

"Yeah, if you go straight and make a right, you will see a coffee dispenser," the custodian said.

"Thanks, appreciate it," Robert said with a slight smile.

Robert dialed his cell phone and called Gabriel. The phone rang three times and went to voicemail. "Hey, I'm just calling to check up on you and Justin. Please, give me a call back bye."

Outside the hospital, Gabriel was alone in the parking lot in his car, drinking beer from a can, listening to his police scanner of criminal activities. He was relaxed and in his own world. Out of nowhere, a black-gloved hand gripped his throat from the back seat, while a machete blade was plunged into the back seat. Gabriel screamed in agony.

The blade penetrated his back through the front, exposing the bloody blade. Blood trickled from his mouth. Then, there was silence after he pulled the blade out. The Masked killer stepped out of the back seat of the car and closed the door. He took Gabriel's head to crave the letter A into his forehead with a box cutter. He wiped the blood off the machete blade with Gabriel's shirt. The Masked killer left the scene while whistling in the silent night.

Chapter 5

Two hours had passed. Robert drove to the Redwood Police Station. As he left his car, rain rippled against his face and clothing, his shoes sloshing against a puddle of water toward the main entrance. Robert pushed through the door, with frowning brows, looking straight through the door with urgency. He walked straight past the lobby, his shoes squeaked on the marble grey floor. The light was beaming above him. Robert felt the warmth from the light. He combed his short hair with his hands. It was difficult for Robert to contain the rage he felt when he discovered Gabriel's savage murder. It was as if an atomic bomb exploded inside his head a billion times.

Entering through the double green doors, Robert noticed a handful of FBI agents circling the precinct. He felt eyes were on him. Silence and eyebrows were raised when Robert walked past them. Some FBI agents were on their laptops, some were on their phones. As he walked down past a crowd of Fed's, Robert found a handful of police officers in an office space sitting in chairs, cooperating with the

FBI, briefing one another on the latest information, and exchanging files that they had that were useful in their investigation.

One of the FBI members dressed in a black suit and black tie was going over the photos of twenty-five victims that were projected on a large computer screen."Okay, people, what do we have on the latest? Do we have anything on this serial killer?"

"There have been five murders in the past five weeks. Each of the victims was local cops and others were their children. Corey White, Jason Diggs, Nathan Ross, Adam Ross, and now Gabriel Logan. Fifteen body parts of victims have been uncovered at a local park site. The killer is meticulous, smart, and likes to set elaborate death traps for his victims. He records the whole experience through a camera feed. This individual seems to cover his tracks well, leaving no fingerprints, or hair. He likes to leave his signature markings of the letter A on the decapitated foreheads, severed hands as his calling cards, and has a need to collect the victim's eyeballs. It has come to my attention that the killer has Jordan Maxwell age twenty-two, his mother Amber Maxwell is missing."

"Okay, why would a killer remove the eyes of the victim and carve a letter on their decapitated heads?" A second FBI agent asked."Why leave the hands?"

"I believe our killer is sending a message," the first FBI agent said, "The killer is asserting power. But there is more. This was a revenge motive. That is why he is targeting men in blue. I'm convinced he will kill again soon. Do you have anything on that camera footage from the parking lot of Gabriel's murder?"

Robert Interrupted. "You are right to think that, but to him, it is a game. He is sending a message to me."

All police and FBI agents turned their attention to Robert standing in the doorway.

"Excuse me, who are you?" One FBI agent asked eyebrows flaring up in annoyance after being interpreted in his presentation.

"Detective, Robert Maxwell."

"Oh, Cambell told me about you. You were suspended from the force. What are you doing here?"

"None of your business. I want to see Captain Cambell. I have no time for games."

"She's not here," the one FBI agent said. "We got the lead on the investigation."

"Who the hell are you?" Robert asked in an angry tone. "I thought Fed's are not supposed to take over cases? We are supposed to work together."

"I'm Director David Swanson. I'm in charge of this operation. We do share our information with state, federal, and local law enforcement. Don't believe what you hear about us from the movies. This particular case is different since we are dealing with a dangerous serial killer. Rest assured we are not taking over your police station. We are here to assist in capturing this suspect."

Robert walked up to David, looking him in the eyes. "This suspect has my son and Amber. He stabbed two of my friends. One is still recovering from his injuries."

"Do you have a problem with me, Detective Maxwell?"

Robert stared at David as if he was a gladiator ready to strike in the arena. "No problem at all."

I pulled up the video, sir," a third FBI agent said. "This is what I was able to pull up from the footage."

A video played, showing Gabriel sitting in his car. It showed him drinking a can of beer. "Can you zoom in and fast forward," David commanded. "Right there, pause that image."

The image showed a man in a gold mask, black sweater, and hoodie with blue jeans coming out of the back seat of the victim's door. They watched the killer with a machete in hand get into a black van and drove off.

"It looks like we got our first image of the killer," David said. "Benson, were you able to get the license plate tags?"

"I manage to get that off the Automated license plate recognition, it will take a few minutes to get the image of the plates through the alphanumeric characters." Robert knew that the Automated License Plate Reader (ALPR) would be a shoe in to track and possibly capture the Masked killer.

Law Enforcement had used this technology to search for vehicles that have been stolen or be involved in criminal or terrorist actions that were owned by the perpetrator. ALPR systems operate on fast cameras. They work to identify character recognition of the license plates and transfer their data software to law enforcement when they get a verified match.

These cameras are staged and attached to light poles, bridges, and overhead signs even on police vehicles. They keep track of the date and time of a vehicle's license plates when passing certain locations.

ALPR systems are able to capture images of at least 1,850 plates per minute at speeds between 125 to 165 miles per hour. ALPR is handy when used to track the location and speed of a vehicle.

"Here we go, sir. License plates are registered to Frank Murdock age 36. He had been arrested for stealing a firearm, assault, and drug possession. His address is 22 Trenton Drive. The vehicle is a Black GMC 2020 van. It was last seen East of Broadway Street and Cooper Ave."

"Good work, Benson. Sound the alert to law enforcement. Tell them not to engage the car, but keep surveillance on him until Agent Milford and Cook arrive."

"You got it, sir," Benson said, getting his radio out to dispatch.

Robert gazed at his image of the Masked killer from the parking lot. His cell phone started to ring. It came from an unknown caller. He answered the phone.

"Hello?"

"Hello, Detective Maxwell. Have you come to your decision?"

Robert paused for a moment to collect himself. He leaned against a table and saw a yellow note pad and black pen."Where do you want to meet?" Robert wrote a message out on the pad and lifted it up to show David that he was talking to the Masked killer.

"Meet me at the warehouse at 9 Pine Street. Come alone. If you don't follow the rules, there will be consequences."

"I want to speak to Jordan and Amber. I need to know they are alive."

The Masked killer leaned the phone to Jordan's ear."Dad!"

"Son, are you okay? Did he hurt you?"

"I'm a little bruised up but I'll live," Jordan said.

"Is your mother with you?"

"I--"

Before Jordan said another word, the Masked killer took the phone away from his ear. "That's all you'll get, Detective Maxwell. Come to the warehouse at 10 pm. I'm looking forward to our next game. See you soon." The Masked killer hung up his cell phone.

"He hung up on me," Robert said.

"Benson, please tell me were you able to trace the call?" David asked.

"No, sir, his call was not traced," Benson said.

"No matter, Agent Milford and Cook will be there to pay a visit to Frank Murdock," David said.

"I'm leaving," Robert said. "If you happen to see Captain Cambell, have her call me."

"Wait, where are you going?" David asked.

"To save my family," Robert said leaving the police station.

"Something is not right about this. Agent Jeremy and Carol I need you to follow Detective Maxwell and report to me on anything you find."

"You got it, boss," Agent Jeremy said leaving the police station with Carson.

David took a moment to look at the image of the Masked killer on screen. "What are we up to? Agent Bridge, I need you to pull up files on Detective Maxwell. I want to know his past cases and send them to my office. There has to be a connection."

"I will get them for you, sir," Bridge said.

David walked to his office and sat on his chair. He went on his laptop and turned it on. David received an email. He opened it. Inside the email, there was a video message and David clicked on the play button.

"I have something that belongs to you," the Masked killer said. The image revealed Captain Cambell in a dark dungeon-like room bound and gagged on a black table with rope. "If you want her alive, you must follow my instructions."

Robert got in his car and took off from the police station. He sped through the highway. A black car tailed him. Robert turned on his radio to listen to music.

"The boss wants us to follow this Maxwell character," Carol said.

"Yeah, it is how it goes. Tell me about Erica, how is she? How long have you been dating her?" Jeremy asked with a smirk.

"Oh, she is fine as hell. We've been dating for nine months now. As you don't know, she is the daughter of John Denver, the District Attorney of Redwood, Washington. I've been hooking up with her a lot. I mean a lot. Believe me, when I say this, Erica can hold her note; she is direct and a screamer. And get this, she is engaged to another guy who is a lawyer."

"I would be careful if I were you. You're playing with fire."

"Playing with fire? I'm okay and besides, her fiance doesn't get what I have."

"What would that be?"

"The right set of tools to do the job."

Jeremy and Carol chuckled.

Robert just pulled up on the curb and parked his car. He got out of the car with his handgun out and headed toward the warehouse. Robert walked on the grass of a wooded area surrounded by trees and bushes. He had no idea what awaited him, or what sick game the Masked killer had in store for him inside the warehouse. His only thought was finding Jordan and Amber.

Robert didn't care about anything else. But, something about this place felt familiar. This would go back twenty years when he was just a rookie cop. He and his partner, Ronald Decan confronted a serial killer named RJ Walters, who was well known for killing and dismembering body parts of men, women, and teenagers of over fifty people. He would embalm them in white wax and rubber to preserve the victims.

The media called him the Mannequin killer until later he was called the Chameleon killer when he dressed his victims after embalming them. It was the place Ronald got killed in the line of duty. That was when Robert comforted and shot RJ five times in the torso and head. To him, it seemed like yesterday. To this moment, the guilt ate him since he couldn't save his partner Ronald. Now, he is forced to enter the place that jump started his career in law enforcement.

Jeremy turned off the headlight from the car to not draw attention. He parked the car five blocks from Robert's car. They both got out of the car and followed him. Unbeknownst to them, something moved in the shadows.

"Okay, we are going in. You cover my back," Jeremy said.

"Alright, I got you covered," Carol said.

The sound of a twig snapped in the woods. "Hey, did you hear something?"Carol asked as he turned around.

"I didn't hear anything. Come on, we have to keep moving to catch up with Robert."

From behind a tree, the Masked killer watched the two agents go inside the warehouse. He took two of his knives out of his sheath and began to walk forward, anticipating their movements.

Jeremy and Carol both entered the warehouse through the rusty door. It was filled with cobwebs and dust inside that was enough to suffocate the surroundings. Fluorescent lights shone above them. Carol passed through the hallway and walked into a room of shelves full of wooden crates stocked left to right. Jeremy entered the room.

"Now where did he go?" Jeremy asked.

"Something doesn't feel right," Carol said.

The lights went out and they were in total darkness.

https://www.youtube.com/watch?v=WV1vhre9BC0

Chapter 6

J eremy and Carol turned on their flashlights. The Masked killer continued to move in the shadows with his blades out. His black-gloved hands gripping the halt. Jeremy paused for a moment. He turned around and pointed his light in front of him, directing the light at the crates. The Masked killer was hiding behind a wooden crate. Jeremy walked forward in that direction. Carol was behind him, covering his back.

"FBI come out with your hands up!" Jeremy said, pointing his gun forward. He walked slowly toward the crates.

The Masked killer was breathing heavily as if he knew his prey was coming to him. Hollow footsteps were approaching the Masked Killer. Before Jeremy went further, he stopped to click his gun. "Come out now with your hands up!"

The Masked killer stood out with blades in hand. He watched Jeremy, studying his movement. His eyes glanced at Carol with his gun pointed to him. He didn't flinch, nor did he back down.

"Get down on your knees and drop your weapon!" Jeremy said.

The Masked killer smirked under his mask. "You have nice eyes. I can't wait to have them. You will make a new edition to my collection. I bet your mother has the same color eyes, or do you get it from your dear old dad." The Masked killer moved backward.

"Don't move! Drop your weapons...I will put you down!" Jeremy said. "There is nowhere to go." Jeremy inched closer. "I'm not gonna ask again, drop your weapons!"

"You think you are in control of the situation," The Masked killer said in a mechanical voice. "Maybe I will pay a visit to your mother. No, I won't take her eyes. I will keep her alive as my personal pet. Yes, she will serve my needs well just like the others."

Jeremy's hands tightened on the gun. His triggered finger was starting to itch. His eyes glaring deep at the Masked killer. As Jeremy stepped forward, the Masked killer pushed down on the hilt of his right blade. An automatic machine gun popped out of a crate from the wall on the right side and opened fire at Jeremy, making him skip from the impact, turning him into a pincushion with armor-piercing rounds of ammo.

Jeremy went down hard on the floor. Carol jumped out of the way from the bullets. Blood gurgled from Jeremey's mouth. He knew his partner was gone and there was nothing he could do for him. Carol took a hit to his arm from the automatic machine gun.

The Masked killer had deactivated the automatic machine gun, pushing the hilt of his blade and he leaned down on Jeremy. "You know, for the record, I let you think you were in control. When you walk into someone's home, they have the home advantage." He patted Jeremy's shoulder letting him choke on his own blood.

Carol started to move on foot; he fired more shots, missing the Masked killer. The Masked Killer walked humming. "I like it when they run."

Carol pushed down some shelves to slow down the Masked killer. "Dammit!" Carol fired his weapon at the Masked killer, nicking his arm. Then, with quick motion, the Masked killer hurled a knife at Carol's hand that carried the gun. Pissed off from the gunshot wound to the arm, he jumped over the shelf, and tackled Carol. In the instant, Carol punched him hard to the face while the Masked killer took a knife to his face, slashing his right cheek. Carol gripped his hand trying to force the blade away from his chest. He countered Carol's attacks and punched him in the jaw.

The Masked killer pushed the blade close to his eye. Carol struggled against the knife. He moved his left leg inward to the side and kicked the Masked killer several times in the nuts. "That's for Jeremy, you bastard!"

The Masked killer moaned and screamed in rage. Carol reversed his position, banging the Masked Killer's hand to drop the knife, while punching him in the face. The Masked killer flung dust to his eyes and punched Carol. He snuck up behind Carol and placed him in a chokehold. "Go to sleep."

Carol moved against the wall and elbowed The Masked killer. He tightened his grip on his neck as Carol resisted. "That's it, let go."

Carol had lost consciousness and went down. The Masked killer picked up Carol and went through a door.

Hours later, Carol woke up in a room disorientated from the pain. His gut felt sore. His arms bound by leather thick straps, laying on a flatbed. He heard someone whistling on the corner of his ear. The Masked killer stood over him. He tilted his head to the side observing him. "Oh, you are awake. It is nice to meet you, Carol, and you work for the FBI. I couldn't have you, or your partner, ruining my plans for my work. So, I am gonna ask some questions and you will answer them honestly. How many agents know about this place? Did you come alone?"

"Jeremy? What have you done with him?" The Masked killer took a knife to his face.

"That is not an answer!" The Masked killer said, pounding his fist on the table. Oh, I wouldn't worry too much about him. I disposed of his body. I am really interested in how you and your partner stumble to my place."

The Masked Killer looked at the video monitor and noticed Robert was moving further in the warehouse. "Well, it looks like I won't have more time to talk to you, Carol." Carol struggled against his restraints. The Masked Killer reached for his syringe and injected a sedative to Carol's right arm.

"My colleagues will come looking for me," Carol said drifting to unconsciousness.

"Sleep well, Carol. I have to go and entertain my guests."

* * *

Meanwhile, Robert walked further inside the warehouse back room. His phone started to ring and he took it up and noticed an unknown caller. He answered the phone after the third ring. He walked slowly, watching all corners for anything.

"Hello," Robert said.

"Hello, Detective Maxwell. I'm so happy you came. Do you remember this place?" the Masked killer inquired.

"Of course, you do remember. This was the same place you and your partner murdered RJ. So, how did it feel to kill the notorious Reaper of Redwood? Hmmm?" The Masked killer asked.

"Enough with the games. I want to see my son Jordan and Amber. Where are they?" Robert demanded.

"Come on, humor me... Did you enjoy killing RJ? I bet you had that same vengeful look when you took his life." The Masked gripped his gloved hand, watching Robert from behind in the shadows. "The way you snuffed out his life like it was nothing. You killed someone important to me. Now, I'll take everything that is important to you, starting with your family."

"You let them go. This is between you and me," Robert said with a defiant tone.

"No, that is not how it works. I want you to suffer. I want you to feel misery and despair for killing RJ!"

"Who is RJ to you?" Robert asked.

"He's my father!" The Masked killer pushed Robert from behind against a create, dropping his cell phone. Robert turned around in time and avoided a knife slash against his chest, dodging it.

The Masked killer kicked the gun out of Robert's hand. He came to Robert with a knife for the second time. Robert grabbed his wrist and arm and twisted it. He flipped the Masked killer over. The Masked killer punched Robert in the stomach, knocking him out of breath. He stood up and punched Robert in the face.

Robert spat out blood from his lips. "That's what this is all about? You are mad because I dusted your daddy?"

The Masked killer screamed, throwing a punch, with glaring eyes at Robert's face, but he countered it and he head-butted the Masked killer.

"You should have never picked a fight with me," Robert said, pounding his face into the crate, breaking his right arm. "Where are they?"

Robert took the Masked killer by the throat, choking him. "Where are they? You will tell me where they are!" The Masked killer flipped Robert over to counter his grip. The Masked killer got up and kicked Robert in the ribs.

"You are getting a slower old man," the Masked killer said in a cold metallic voice kicking him in the stomach. He went over to pick up his knife and walked over to Robert. The Masked killer walked slowly to Robert. In desperation, Robert was crawling on the floor for the gun that was five inches from him.

"I can't wait to do some work with you, Robert. You will make a great masterpiece for my work. It is a shame it had to end this way." The Masked killer moved his knife in position ready to plunge it to Robert.

Out of nowhere, a squadron of FBI agents waltzed in the ware-house with guns. "FBI drop your weapon now!"

"Drop the knife and raise your hands!" The FBI agent repeated. "If you don't do it, we will light your ass up."

The Masked dropped the knife and his hands were raised. One FBI agent put handcuffs on him. He looked at Robert and said, "This isn't over Detective Maxwell, I still have your family." The Masked killer laughed while being dragged out of the warehouse. Robert came at him with rage in his eyes. Two FBI agents pulled him off the Masked killer.

"Where are they?" Robert asked.

The Masked killer laughed. "That's not how the game is played."

"Get this creep out of here before I put a bullet into him myself," One FBI agent said.

"My you have nice eyes. I can't wait to have them," the Masked Killer said to the FBI agent.

"Get him out of here!" The FBI agent said. "Hey, are you okay?"

"Okay? That monster has my family. I want answers," Robert said bumping against his shoulder.

Hours had passed, Robert was back at the police station. This time he watched from the monitors of the interrogation room. Robert squinted his eyes. David Swanson was the one, grilling the Masked killer's confession and whereabouts of the Maxwell family. Even though it lasted for two hours.

The Masked Killer never spoke. He was handcuffed to a poll lis-tening to David's monologue. The Masked killer ignored David and looked through the mirror as if he sensed Robert was looking at him. He waved at the mirror with his right hand.

David placed photos of twenty victims that the Masked killer had killed in front of him. "Is this supposed to mean something?"

"Look at the pictures! Take a good look! I want to know. Where is Captain Cambell? Tell me the other victim's location?"

The Masked Killer looked straight at David like he was nothing and took his time to admire his watch. David slammed his hand on the table. "I'm talking to you!"

The Masked killer pressed a button on his watch. Screams and gunfire were heard from the halls. Robert left the room and noticed a handful of black drones, moving in unison, busting through windows with automatic machine guns, mowing down both FBI and policemen and women. Bodies and blood soiled the ground.

The police and FBI that were left standing started to fire on the drones with their handguns and shotguns. Some of the drones went down but they were overwhelmed by the magnitude of drones popping in.

"Get the hell out of here!" Robert said, firing his handgun at one of the black drones. He went inside the interrogation room.

When the police and FBI raced to the door, they discovered they were locked. Panic and fear were written on their faces.

Robert grabbed the Masked killer by the throat and pushed his body against the table. "Call them off!"

"The game is not over yet, Detective Maxwell," The Masked killer said, pressing the button on his watch again, causing the drones to self-destruct, blowing up the remaining FBI and policemen. Their screams were muffled by the sound of the explosion. Smoke engulfed the hallway.

Robert and David turned around for a moment and walked out of the room to witness the carnage that took place. Arms and other limbs were scattered across the room.

"Shit!" David said as his eyes widened, his eyebrows arched at the horrors he witnessed.

The Masked killer picked the handcuffs with a black hairpin hidden in his right glove. He snatched up David's handgun from his holster and knocked out Robert. David felt a cold tip of metallic steel against the back of his head. He turned around with his hands up to face the Masked killer.

"Wait, we had a deal!" David shouted.

"Deals off," the Masked killer said, shooting David in the head. He fell on the left, laying on the side.

"Until we meet again, Robert. The game is far from over," the Masked killer said.

Chapter 7

- -

J ordan awoke tied in the black rope around the waist, sitting in a chair. A black lamp gave a mild glow that reflected the white walls. His head hurt from being drugged. Jordan's vision came to focus. He noticed his right arm was sore with small cuts. The cuts were deep with a small A symbol mark. Jordan looked all around and noticed a painting of an image of a black and white photo contrast of a man.

A brown cabinet that had thick books that look like encyclopedias piqued Jordan's curiosity. He needed access to a working phone to call the police. Figuring out how to escape the room, won't be an easy task. He knew that deep down inside. Thinking about his son Kevin and girlfriend Jennifer was his motivation to break out of this place.

On the far corner of the right, he saw a 32" flat-screen TV set on a brown table. Jordan glanced to his left and saw Sam by a wooden table on a chair, eating a bowl of cereal. The clinking noise of the spoon and smacking noise of Sam's lips confirmed his observations. His only chance of escape was to win Sam's trust.

"Hi, Sam. How are you, buddy!"

Sam put down his bowl of cereal, got up from the chair, and ran toward Jordan. "Hey, Jordan, I am so happy you are awake!" Sam said with a smile.

"I'm kinda hungry. Do you have any food I can eat?"

"Yeah, I can get you some cereal. I promise I won't let him hurt you." He gets a bowl of cereal and pores in the milk. Sam gives Jordan a bowl of cereal with a spoon.

"So, Sam, how did you end up here?"

"The man in the Mask took care of me."

"What happened to your parents?"

"They died," Sam said in a sad tone looking down at the floor.

"I know you must miss them," Jordan said with an empathetic tone.

Sam changed the subject to lighten the mood."Hey, do you want to play a game with me? I got toys." Sam went to his toy chest and opened a box.

Jordan smiled and replied, "Sure, we can play a game. Go ahead and get your toys."

Sam moved fast and slid a small wooden table close to Jordan. He smiled at Jordan.

"I got something for you," Sam said, revealing two Hot Wheel cars. One is a black 69' Ford Mustang with a red 2007 Ford Mustang. Sam gave Jordan the red Mustang and Sam took the black Mustang.

"So, you like to play with cars?" Jordan asked.

"Yeah, I love cars. I have a whole collection of different cars," Sam said, guiding his black car on the table with his hand.

"Thanks for playing with me. I don't have a lot of friends. I missed Joey. He was really nice."

"What happened to Joey?"

Sam grew silent and looked at Jardon with sad eyes to confirm his suspicion that he didn't return. "I'm sorry, I know you miss him."

"There is nothing to be sorry about your friend," Jordan said with a reassuring stare.

Sam hugged Jordans. "I promise I won't let the sad man hurt you."

Heavy footsteps were heard outside the door. The door opened, letting out a slight screech. The Masked Killer entered the room. His dark gloved right hand tightened. He kicked the table down. Sam was startled by his intrusion as he stepped back.

"What are you doing here? Get back to your room!" The Masked killer said.

"But I was just playing a game," Sam said.

"I said get back to your room!" The Masked killer said, pulling Sam by the arm, opening the door and pushing him out. He fell on the floor face first.

The Masked killer closed the door and locked it. "Hello, Jordan I saw your father."

Sam got up and ran to the door and he looked through a keyhole. The Masked killer pulled up a chair in front of Jordan. His left foot tapped on the wooden floor.

"Would you like some tea? I'm sure you are thirsty," the Masked killer said. "I have green tea."

"No, I don't want your damn tea!" Jordan said.

"I see where you got your temper from. Like father, like son," the Masked killer said. "He put up quite a show at the police station."

Jordan flinched against his restraints, hissing at the Masked killer. "I see the fire in those eyes. They would make a good collection piece."

The Masked killer took out his signature knife. He held it close to Jordan's arm. "What are you doing?"

"I'm just having a little time. Plus, I want to make your father suffer for what he did to me and my family."

"What does that have to do with me?"

The Masked killer kicked the table down. "It has everything to do with you!" He puts the blade against Jordan's throat. His cold eyes bulged out, waiting to slit his throat.

"I should kill you now, but I have plans for you. Just wait, you will see. It will be something you will never forget. I want to see the look on your father's face when I snuff out your life. It will be glorious to see."

The Masked killer got up from Jordan's arm and turned on the light. Jordan's eyes hardened. Over to his right, he saw gift-wrapped boxes in red colors. From the top that was exposed, contained remnants of heads, arms, and hands. Each of the body parts was covered in wax-like rubber preserved in formaldehyde.

"Do you see my special work? I was planning on emailing them to your father." Then, once I do that. I was gonna pay a visit to your girlfriend."

Jordan's eyes glared as he pulled against his restraints. "You stay away from her! If you touch her, I will kill you!"

The Masked killer laughed. "You think I'm gonna kill her? No, she will not die. In fact, she will serve another purpose."

"Since we are going to be spending quality time together, I would like to get to know you more."

"You can go to hell," Jordan said.

"If you want to do things the hard way, we can do that too," the Masked killer said.

The Masked killer reached for his remote control from his pocket. He pressed the button to turn on the lights. Jordan noticed a glass display of men and women well dressed preserved in formaldehyde, rubber, and wax. Their eyes, missing from their sockets.

"Do you like my work?" The Masked killer asked.

Jordan started to throw up on the floor.

"That's right, Jordan, let it all out," the Masked killer said.

Jordan's head came up for air. "You are a sick man."

"This is my masterpiece, but I'm missing some parts," the Masked killer said.

"My father will find you. When he does, he will kill you," Jordan said.

"I don't think so, Jordan," the Masked Killer said. "All that your father will find will be bread crumbs I left for him."

The Masked killer took out his black cell phone and snapped a portrait of Jordan."I want to savor this moment."

The Masked killer picked up his black controller from his pocket and pushed the button. Bright lights came on to blind Jordan's sight with great intensity. Jordan closed his eyes. "Light that burns so bright at every sight. Must be out of sight." Wouldn't you say so, Jordan?"

"Please, turn off the lights," Jordan said. Jordan closed his eyes.

"Now, where is the fun in that," the Masked killer said.

"If you excuse me, I have to go and retrieve my new masterpiece. Do I have to know? Does Jennifer like to wear red or blue?"

"You stay away from her!" Jordan said eyes bulged. His wrist tightened. "If you touch her, I will kill with my bare hands. I will kill you--Do you hear me!"

"I'm just getting started. We are gonna spend some quality time together. It's nice to see I get a rise out of you. Your suffering is just the beginning. First, I need to break you. Then, the healing will start. You will learn to see things my way."

"I'm not gonna play your sick games," Jordan said. "You can go to hell."

"Oh, you will, you will play!" The Masked killer said. "I'm going to take you in my image." The Masked killer placed a gage over his mouth. "That will shut you up!"

The Masked killer walked out of the room, closing the door on Jordan. Jordan screamed, wiggling from the chair side to side. The Masked killer laughed at his despair.

The Masked killer checks under the table. "Sam," get over here now."

Sam hid behind a shelf in another room. The Masked killer walked the hallway slowly in the shadows Sam kept on moving. He ran down the stairs toward the cellar. Sam struggled to lift a small piece of wood off the floor. He went inside the hole. Sam sealed the wood above him. He heard footsteps above him. He didn't make a sound.

"Sam!" Where are you, boy?" The Masked killer asked kicking the tables and pushing shelves on the floor.

"Sam! Sam! I know you are in here," The Masked killer said. "I just want to talk. I promise I won't hurt you."

Sam heard him talk and kept quiet, hoping the Masked killer would go away."

The Masked killer went down to the cellar door and opened it. He saw the bed and lifted up the mattress and threw it back down. Sam was shivering in terror. The Masked killer was standing over the wood that Sam hid under. Sam closed his eyes and hoped that the Masked Killer wouldn't find him there.

"Last chance, come out now!" The Masked killer said with a loud tone.

There was a sudden knock from outside the house. The Masked killer heard it. Jordan heard it and tried to scream. The Masked killer gasped and went back up the steps and took off his mask. When he went to the door, he looked through the small glass window, a man standing in front of the door. His hand gripped the blade behind his back. He opened the door.

"Oh, hey, Charles, long time no see. What brings you here?"

"Nothing much, Devin, I'm just stopping by. I haven't seen in a while what have you been doing lately?"

Devin tightened his knife again behind his back and smiled at Charles. "I have been working on an art project.Abstract work you know." His hand tightened on the blade behind the door.

"Oh, maybe you can show me," Charles said, trying to push through the door. Devin pushed back.

"Now wouldn't be a good time," Devin said with a fake smile. When are you free? I can invite you over next week. How does Friday sound?"

Charles looked at him with a warm smile and shook his hand. "Next week it is."

"Well, I better let you get back to it then," Charles said, his eyes focused on Devin's facial expression.

"Yeah, thanks for stopping by," Devin said. He waved at him. Devin gave a fake smile that took effort.

Charles turned around and headed to his car. Devin closed the door and put on the deadbolt. He leaned against the door, sighing. He knew if Charles set foot inside his house, he would be dead. For years, Devin has been keeping watch on Charles. He knew his father was a cop. A cop was responsible for the death of his father just like Robert. One by one, Devin had a playbook on how he was going to carry out his sick game to entertain his fantasies. For five years, he had planned for this moment.

Devin went back to the cellular to check on Sam. He called out to Sam and there was no reply. Then, he looked down and noticed a small gap in the wooden frame of the floor. He pulled it up. Devin reached in through the dark floor and felt nothing. His face lit up.

Charles's car started and took off from Devin's home. Sam was inside his car, hiding under the camping blanket in the back seat. He didn't make any sound. Sam was lucky to sneak out of the cellar by going through a trap door Devin didn't know about.

By the time Devin ran out of the house, Charles was already long gone. Devin punched the corner of the house in frustration. His teeth gritted together, holding back the moisture of his tongue, letting out a loud bellow sound from his mouth.

Devin sighed and collected himself. He thought to himself, "I need to get Sam back. He will be back. After all, he is my nephew. And family doesn't abandon family. Don't worry, Charles, you won't get far. I have other plans for you. But for right now, I have to check on Detective Robert Maxwell. The game has to go on."

Chapter 8

O utside of the Redwood Police Department, the sound of sirens surrounded the area. Smoke covered the air inside the building. Robert woke up from the floor barely conscious. He coughed as he stood up, leaning against the wall. Robert glanced at David Swanson's body sprawled out on the floor. His arms out-stretched with a large gap from the side of his head. Since most of his head was blown clear off, Robert knew he was dead. He continued to walk through the eviscerated body parts of his fellow police officers and FBI agents splattered on the right corner of his vision. His head throbbed from the impact he received from being knocked out from the back of the head. With each movement, blood trickled on the side of his face.

Rest in peace, David, "Robert said, wincing from his head injury. "I didn't like you anyway."

Robert had to leave the police station. His only concern was pro-tecting Jennifer and his grandchild. He had a feeling that the Masked Killer would go after them just to get back at him.

Robert reached for his cell phone and made a call as he strode through the halls.

"Hello," she said.

"Jen, it's Robert, are you home?" Robert asked.

"Yes, Robert, what's wrong?" Jennifer questioned.

"I want you to do something for me. I need you to lock your doors. Don't open the door for anyone until I get there, "Robert said with a serious tone.

"Robert, what's going on?" Jennifer inquired.

Robert ended the phone call. He heard banging from outside. "Is anyone in there?"

Robert went further up to see who it was. There was a man in a dark Fireman suit, peeping through the window of the entrance.

"I am here!" Robert yelled back.

Robert walked over more corpses of officers. He went through the hallway. An explosion took place that caused part of the ceiling to collapse in front of the main entrance. It spread from the ceiling and walls, blocking Robert's path. The intensity of the heart increased, causing Robert to retract back with his arm over his mouth. The bodies of the fallen police roasted in flames. There was nothing he could do for them.

Robert's option was to find another alternative to escape. He thought of one exit in the back. Robert strode back to that exit fast. He noticed a door that was free from blockage. As Robert reached for the doorknob, he realized that it was locked. Robert took out his gun and aimed it at the door. He fired three shots. Then he kicked at the door as hard as he could. Frustration built up as Robert did it again and the door didn't budge. He kicked hard at the door four times until it gave in.

"Of course, he didn't make it easy for me," Robert said. "When I get out here, I'm gunning for his ass. I will make him pay for what he did."

Robert ran down the steps, holding onto the metal railing. He heard helicopters from outside. "Just a couple more steps and I'm home free."

Robert went through the door away from the Police Department to get some air. When Robert walked away from the building, it exploded. A fire roared through the broken glass of the building. The fire spread faster toward the roof, releasing more smoke.

"Well, good thing I got out in time," Robert said as he pulled out his cigarette and put it in his mouth. He reached for his silver lighter. He stared at the burning huffing and puffing smoke from his cigarette.

Robert's cell phone rang again. When Robert looked at the ID, it was unknown.

"Hello, Detective Maxwell, I see you survived my explosive booby trap," Devin said. "I am glad you did survive. Now the game will start soon."

"You won't get away with this you bastard! Oh, there will be a manhunt for your ass and I will be the first in line to cap you."

Devin laughed. "Killing all those feds and police officers as part of the plan. No, detective. I will be the one to kill you when the time is right."

"We will see about that," Robert said, hanging up the phone.

The Police Department roared with another massive explosion, destroying the building. It pushed back firefighters and policemen that arrived at the scene from the other side of the building. Robert flicked his cigarette, ran to his Jaguar, and got inside the car that smelled of fresh clean linen scent. He turned on the ignition, set the gear in reverse, switched the gear to drive while punching down on the accelerator. He made a wide turn out of the parking lot. Robert drove forward. He served on the open road, going beyond 55 mph. He thought about one thing. That was getting to Jennifer before the Masked killer did.

Robert glanced behind him for a second through the mirror to make sure he wasn't followed. The last thing he needed was to be followed by anyone.

"Hold on, Jennifer! I'm on my way," Robert said, taking a detour off an exit.

Robert passed the cemetery. He knew he was almost close to Jennifer's house. He got a call from his Bluetooth. He saw the name come up on his display screen. He answered from his wheel.

"Hey, Kenny," Robert said.

"I just saw the evening news about the explosion at the Police Department. I was hoping you were not inside that building "Are you okay?"

"Been better, how are you holding up?" Robert asked.

"Well, doing good. I'm about to be discharged from the hospital," Kenny said. "The doctors here stitched me up real good."

"That's good to hear, Kenny. I am glad you are okay," Robert said with an optimistic tone.

Kenny paused."Robert, are you sure you are okay, you seem."

"I'm fine. That psychopath is still out there and still has my boy and Amber. I'm heading over to Jennifer's house to keep her and my grandson safe. I will talk to you later," Robert said.

"Hey, if you need anything," Kenny said.

"I appreciate it, Kenny," Robert said.

"I'm serious. Call me, if you need anything," Kenny mentioned.

"Okay, Kenny take care!" Robert said.

Robert drove past the fog that appeared around the corner. He made a hard turn when a deer ran in front of the road. Robert smashed his foot on the brakes. He gritted his teeth, banged his hand on the steering wheel, as the deer moved out of the road in haste. The deer managed to meet up with a horde of deer. Robert took another breath and turned his head to see if his path was cleared.

Robert had a million things going through his mind. He rolled down the window to get some air. Robert wondered if his son was okay? Did that psycho hurt him? Where would he hide him? Even though Jordan and Robert argue back and forth, he still loved him and would do anything to get him back. No longer how long it takes. One thing is certain, Robert was hell-bent on finding him.

In less than ten minutes, Robert arrived at Jennifer's brown house, parking his car behind her car in the driveway. He noticed the panels of the roof had solar panels with red and black roofing. The lights were on at the front porch. Robert got out of the car and strode to the front door. He stepped on the brown welcome mat, knocking on the door hard with three taps.

Jennifer went to the door and checked through the window to see it was Robert. She removed the deadbolts on the door and chain fast. Jennifer opened the door, letting out a slight squeak.

"Robert!" Jennifer said, hugging him.

"I saw what happened on the news," Jennifer said. "Oh, you're bleeding? Come on in."She closed the door behind him and locked it.

Robert stared into her eyes, trying to forget the horrors of the Police Department. His mind drifted back to the shock and trauma for a moment, remembering all the blood and carnage he witnessed first hand. He shook his hand, getting back to reality.

Robert followed Jennifer and took his time to look around the house since it was his first time in her home. He looked around at the photos of Jordan and Jennifer together. Then, he turned to his right and see's a baby photo of his grandson, Kevin. A small smile kept on his face, admiring the bundle of joy. He never thought he would be a grandfather at the age of forty-five. Robert thought he failed as a husband to his former wife Amber. How he missed so much of Jordan's life, growing up to become a young man of his own. He would like to try to be a part of Jordan's life and to be able to spend time with his grandson.

Amber, on the other hand, saw Robert as an alcoholic, philander, and at times over the edge. Once Amber caught him in the act with one of the young blonde police cadets, it was over before he was hit hard with divorce papers within a year after their separation. Robert sent her letters and even tried getting on board with marriage counseling, but it was not enough and Amber wanted out.

"I'm sorry, you wouldn't by any chance have an ice pack on you? Would you?" Robert asked.

"Yeah, I can get you one," Jennifer said, heading to the kitchen. "You can sit by the couch." Robert nodded.

Robert ended up on the black leather couch, laying his head back. He touched the back of the head and felt a lump. Robert's head stung worse than a bee sting. He blinked his eyes for a moment. The one thing that bothered Robert was the black Kitty-cat clock that was on the wall. Its yellow eyes moved back and forth. He thought it resembled Felix the cat.

"Where is Kevin?" Robert asked.

"He's asleep in his bed," Jennifer comes to the living room with an ice pack. She hands it to Robert.

"I have reasons to believe the killer is coming for you next. That's why I'm here to protect both of you. I need you to pack your things."

"Okay, I just need to make a couple of phone calls," Jennifer said she had her cell phone on speed dial.

Robert put the ice pack down on the wooden counter and stood up in front of her with a deadpan expression. "No, no one must know where you are, or where you are going. The less they know the better."

Jennifer hung up the cell phone. "I was just gonna call my mother."

Robert interrupted, "That would not be a good idea. For one, this killer will find out where she lives and he'll kill everyone you are close to. Trust me, you are safer with me."

"How do I know that you are not the killer, hmm?" Jennifer asked with her arms folded.

Robert sighed. "You can't be serious! I just lost maybe 150 people tonight. Half of the people I knew were from the force...I witnessed people getting shot to death and blown up! Do you really want that? I know I wouldn't. I'm here to get my grandson and you to safety, that's all that matters right now." Robert pointed his finger to the wall.

"Yeah, and what about Jordan?" Jennifer asked. "Doesn't he matter?"

"Of course, he does. I have spent weeks trying to find him and Amber. I'm not giving up on that. I just don't want to lose any more people tonight. Robert's lips parted, letting out air through them. He took a deep breath.

Robert grabbed her shoulders. "Look, I'm sorry I went off on you. It has been a rough night. Please, Jennifer, your life and the safety of my grandson are on the line here. I promise myself; I don't want to let anyone else become a victim to this killer. All I need you to do is stay at a safe house. It will be for a couple of weeks. You won't be alone. I have people that will look after you."

"Okay, I will get my things," Jennifer said.

"Alright, I will wait for you," Robert said.

Jennifer left to get her things and her grandson. Robert made a call to Kenny. "Hey, it looks like I would need that favor from you after all."

Chapter 9

"Amber, oh Amber! Wake up!" Devin said, yelling at her ear. Pulling the brown blanket from her bed.

Amber got up from the bed in shock. Her body fidgeted against the wall. Her eyes flowed down with tears. Her teeth chattered together, hoping what she experienced wasn't a nightmare. The chain on her right foot restricted her movement.

"Hello Amber," Devin said, caressing her hair with his fingers. Her face echoed with sobbing cries. "So, pretty." Devin squatted down and smelled her neck, savoring her scent. "God, you smell so good. I can see why Robert was so fond of you."

Amber gasped at the sight of his mischievous smirk and pulled away. "Why are you doing this?"

Devin stopped back without losing his gaze on her. "You remind me of someone. She was pretty like you. But she had a lot of mouths. Betrayed my trust." Devin punched his hand against the wall above her head. "You wouldn't betray me would you?"

Devin pulled her head back, hearing Amber sobs getting louder. Her lips curled up in disgust. "I want you to meet her."

Devin pulled out his black controller by hand and pressed a button. In the instant, a light shone at the stool of a severed head. It was a brunette woman covered in formaldehyde, rubber, and yellow wax. Her brown eyes, staring straight at Amber. Her mouth closed as if it was a doll.

"Oh, no!" Amber said.

"You see Linda here thought she could disobey me and not suffer the consequences." Devein continued, "But she learned the hard way. Didn't you, Linda."

Devin picked up her head from the stool and brought it to Amber inches away from her face. "Isn't she pretty? She was a real estate agent. I met Linda in one of the lowest moments in my life. That was right before I got into my projects. I thought I could have a normal life with her. Someone I could one day build a family with! For a moment, I didn't have this need to kill Amber. I was once happy. But Linda ruined everything when she went into my basement. I told her specifically to stay out of the basement! She was insistent to uncover what I was hiding in that basement. I told her, I told her again, I was working on a special project and I wasn't ready to show her my latest work yet until it was done. She didn't listen. So, when Linda went into my basement, she saw my latest masterpiece of a man and woman on my display tables. They were all well preserved. But since Linda saw everything, she had to be dealt with. It was harder on me than on her. You see, Amber, I am an artist. I like to work with my hands. I have done many paintings, sculptures, and mannequins. I like to include the selected view to see my work. Only if you follow my rules. Do you think you can do that? It would be a shame if you didn't follow my rules."

"So, you are the "Mannequin Killer of Redwood?"

Devin smiled. "How astute of you." Devin flashed a grin on his face. He tossed Linda's head to the corner. Devin rubbed Amber's face as it was cream. "I think I will keep you around. I might even let you see your son, Jordan if you behave yourself."

"Jordan, he is here! Please, don't hurt my son," Amber said, pleading to Devin in a subtle tone.

His fingers glided to her check bone like it was clay. "Yeah, I think I will keep you here until you can earn my trust. Trust is a two-way street as they say." Devin whispered in her ear. "I just hope you won't disappoint me. I have to take a road trip to see your ex-husband, Robert. The game is getting very interesting. Soon you and your son will be reunited like a happy family."

"Jordan? He is here? Please, don't hurt him!"

Devin tilted his head observing her.

"I will do anything you won't just don't hurt him," Amber said with sincerity in her eyes. "Please, he is all I got!"

Devin walked out of the room and closed the door behind him. All he heard was Amber's screams across the halls. While walking in the hallway, Devin placed his black controller on the top shelf from the corner of the door that was two blocks from Jennifer's cell. He reached for his bottle of water from the shelf, guzzling it down like no tomorrow. He wiped his lips and tossed the empty bottle into his recycling bin by the floor. Devin went inside his control room. In the room, there were twenty monitors in front of him. He had installed thirty cameras from outside his house to his backyard.

These three people approached his property from the backyard on their bicycles. Each of them kicked on their kickstands for support. Devin cold eyes, glaring at the monitor as he gripped his hand on the table. He stood and grabbed his golden mask, and pulled open a drawer to get his knife. The blade sparkled against his reflection.

"Come on, Jamie, this place must be loaded with stuff," Toad said.

"I don't know, Toad? I don't feel good about this," Jamie said.

"Bro, you can't just walk away. Think of the amount of money, jewels, and other things we get from that place. Plus, think of all the chicks you can get with after. Like that girl, fine girl April. You can buy that car and take her out on a date. What do you say about that?" Zack elbowed his arm and winked.

Jamie rolled his eyes and sighed. "Fine, I'm in. But we get in and get out. This will be the last one."

Devin watched them behind the trees, breathing hard, flexing his fingers. Cold vapors escaping his mouth. "This will be interesting." Devin took out his remote controller and pushed the button until it turned green.

A door opened from the backyard of the house, releasing five German Shepherds with brown and black fur. They ran to their direction. Jamie, Toad, and Zack were startled by the loud barking. One of the German Shepherds paused with Sharp teeth as it growled at the group, dripping spit from Its mouth. When Jamie stopped moving, he saw another one behind him. The other German Shepherds surrounded them with their deep growls and teeth, showing.

"Don't make eye contact with them. Don't move," Jamie said with his hands up.

"Shit! We got to get inside that house!" Zack said with his hands up.

"What are we gonna do?" Toad asked, feeling fearful of dogs closing in.

"I got an idea," Jamie said, picking up a stick. "I will keep them busy. You two-run inside the house."

"What? It's insane these dogs will tear you apart!" Zack said.

Jamie thought it would give them a chance for them to break in while he distracted the dogs. He jumped on the bike, kicked the kickstand, and started pedaling. Jamie cursed under his breath. The dogs barked, running in pursuit of him. One of the dogs jumped up in mid-air from the side. Jamie whacked the dog in the head with his stick. A whipping cry was heard from one dog.

Zack and Toad were five feet from the house. They ran toward the steps to the front door. Toad took out his black key, picking at the lock. He fiddled with the key and dropped on the floor. His hands shook.

"Hurry up!" Zack said.

"I am!" Toad said, trying to turn against the mechanism of the door.

There was a sudden click "I got it." They both entered inside, closing the door.

Jamie kept on riding and entered into a large corn crop in the field. He heard the dogs barking behind him. He got off his bike and hid in a large ditch. Jamie covered his body in the dirt as fast as possible, hoping to drive his scent away from the dogs. The dogs were getting closer and he held his breath.

The dogs were close, sniffing at the ground. The dogs growled as it was closing on Jamie. Jamie closed his eyes and prayed the dogs wouldn't find him. The dogs stopped moving and were called back by Devin's whistle.

Devin petted each of the dog's heads and showed affection for them. "Good boy! You all did well. I'm gonna fix you guys a nice treat at the house. Yes, I am--Come!"

The dogs left the cornfield with Devin. Jamie waited for a moment to peek his head out of the ground through the dirt. He let in the air into his lungs. Jamie crawled out of the ditch. He took a moment to breathe in more of the cold air.

When he stood up in the cornfield, Jamie thought he heard a noise. Jamie treaded close to the corn crops, dangling beside him, and hid. Jamie glanced around, wiping the dirt from his eyes.

"Thank God!" Jamie said.

Devin was behind him in the cornfield. He pulled out a knife and plunged it to Jamie's lower back. Jamie hollered in agony as he went down on the ground. The blade embedded deep into his back, he crawled on the ground with his arms. He looked at Devin, approaching him with his golden mask.

Jamie screamed for help. "No one can hear you!" Devin said.

Devin whistled the dogs to come back to the cornfield. Five dogs circled Jamie, barking louder with white sharp teeth. Their brown eyes, glaring down at him like a meal ticket. Jamie tried to crawl away.

"You hurt one of my dogs. You will pay for that. Alright, boys dinner time!" Devin said, waving his hand.

One German Shepherd clumped down on Jamie's throat. The others started attacking his arms and legs. Screams were heard when Jamie tried to fight them off with his hands. But it wasn't enough and Jamie was torn apart by their jaws. Blood splattered across the cornfield. Devin headed back to his house.

Meanwhile, Toad and Zack explored Devin's house. They came across rare paintings of abstract art and cabinets made in mahogany wood. Toad opened one drawer and found tons of golden Rolex watches.

"Jamie should be back already," Toad said. "This place is loaded with some serious stuff. These Rolex watches will make us rich. Especially the Rolex Submariner 6358."

"Check this out." Toad said, pointing his finger. "This is the watch James Bond used in one of his spy missions. You know the actor Timothy Dalton, who played Bond in License to Kill."

"It's probably a fake anyway," Zack said.

"Wait! Did you hear something?" Toad.

Toad strode through the hallway, staying close to the wall. He reached for a brown door, twisting the doorknob in a slow fashion. Toad felt cold air hit his face. When he walked further into the steel room, and flicked on the light switch from the corner, Toad fell on his knees and started to throw up.

Zack walked in and saw bodies of men and women on tables but in pieces. Zack picked up Toad and suggested to him to get out of the house. Before they made their bold move, a door opened from outside. Devin walked in eager to meet his other guest.

"We got to hide!" Toad whispered.

He took Zack under his arm and moved quickly toward the door leading to a wine cellar. They both went down the concrete stairs and hid behind wine cellar racks further in the back of a brick wall. Devin walked slowly looking around. He noticed his door was left open and felt a cool breeze coming from his kill room. A cold mist escaped the room, spreading throughout the floor. Devin closed the door, preserving his work. He suspected others were close by. Devin closed the drawer that had his Rolex watches and pulled out his knife.

"Don't make a sound," Toad said.

Devin searched all around the house. He heard Jordan in the other room. Devin opened the door to his private room that had several flat-screen monitors, which covered the whole house. He looked through the recordings of the last fifteen minutes of each room. Then, he spotted Toad and Zack. His eyes lit up in excitement, curling his fingers on the hilt of the blade. He left the control room. Devin took his time, going through every door.

"I know you are in here," Devin said. "Why don't you come out and save me the trouble of finding you."

Zack and Toad kept quiet. Their hands poised against the wall.

"Okay, if that's the way you want to play it!" Devin replied.

Devin checked all the rooms. All that remained was his personal wine cellar. Devin opened the door and went down the hollowed concrete steps. Zack and Toad kept silent, making no movements. Toad thought this was it, this was the end.

Chapter 10

Within thirty minutes, trepidation was written between Toad and Zack's faces as Devin searched the area of the wine cellar. Zack glanced around his surroundings, trying to find anything as a weapon. The thumping sound got louder when Devin checked the first row to the second row. He curved his knife and was ready to carve his latest prey into his private collection of body parts. Devin tilted his head to the side, sensing they were cornered. They were soon to be his new edition to his collection. A well-preserved collection like the others before him. And the prize would be their very eyes.

Zack picked up a wine bottle off the shelf and put his finger against his mouth to signal Toad not to move. Zack's stomach tightened in fear as his fist clenched. Cold sweat dripped off Toad's face. He closed his eyes for a split second and took a breath. Footsteps moved closer to his direction. The moment of truth came at hand. It was do or die at that point.

"I am gonna push the shelf down on him and bash his head in with this," Zack whispered. "You run for the door. I'll be right behind you."

"Okay, "Toad said back, nodding his head.

"I know you are in here!" Devin said, scratching the blade against the wall with slow grace. "It is only a matter of time until I get you."

"Shit! He is closing in!" Toad said.

"Okay, run to the side on three!" Zack said with a hand signal. "One...Two...Three!"

Zack pushed the shelf down on Devin as Toad paced up the stairs. Devin's eyes bulged as he dodged the shelf only to get a bottle to the face. Devin swayed his knife side to side, cutting Zack's right hand. Zack lunged back. Devin inched closer with his knife.

"Don't worry, I will take care of you as I did to your friend out in the cornfield. Well, not in the same fashion. My dogs had themselves a great fest," Devin said. "You two will be well preserved in my special project."

Zack looked to his right and picked a long pipe on the floor to defend himself. "You killed Jamie! I will kill you!"

"You got some courage, but it won't be--enough," Devin said.

Unbeknownst to them, Toad jumped Devin from behind pushing him against the wine shelves. Devin punched Toad in the face and kicked him in the chest forcing him to fall on his back. He grabbed him by the collar of his blue shirt, stabbing his shoulder. Toad screamed in anguish. He pushed the blade deeper to make him suffer. Devin punched him in the face, again and again, trying to beat him to the point of death with his fist.

Zack swung his metal pipe against Devin's face from the side, hitting him hard. He kicked him in the stomach. "That's for, Jamie!" Devin grabbed hold of Zack's leg, yanked him to the floor. His hands were around Zack's neck as he tightened his grip, choking the life out of him.

Zack gasped for air, holding on to dear life. He held his hands against Devin, trying to get his hands off his throat. His eyes fluttered upward. Toad got up dazed and he picked up the metal pipe from the corner with one hand. Toad strode over to Devin.

"It won't be long now. Just let go. That's it. Let go!" Devin said, squeezing hard, cutting off Zack's airways.

"Get the fuck off him!" Toad said, hitting Devin in the head twice.

Devin went down and was unconscious. Zack couched wheezing hard. Toad took his hand, pulling him up from the floor while he grimaced.

"Let's get the hell out of here," Toad said.

Toad and Zack ran up the stairs. They both ran through the whole hallway that seemed like an endless maze of rooms. White doors were on each side. Zack tried the doors closed to him, twisting the knobs, but they were locked. Toad's arm left a trail of blood. The blade was still embedded deep into his arm.

Zack clenched his teeth with a frown. "Dammit!"

Toad took out the blade and dropped it. He cursed under his breath. Toad moaned in agony. At the instant, Zack tore off a piece of fabric from his shirt and wrapped it around Toad's arm to stop the bleeding. Toad grimaces from the pain.

Zack picked up the bloody knife.

Toad tried the door in the corner. It was unlocked. A glamour of hope formed on his face. "This way!"

Toad and Zack entered a room surrounded by Mannequins stuffed in large red and blue boxes in each corner. Yet they looked alive. The smell alone repulsed them. That made Toad wheezed hard. Zack looked around and noticed photos of men and women in black and white. All of them were taken in the postmortem.

The images left a morbid feeling of dread. A sickening sense of death was around them. In an instant, all hope pointed to the window above them. Toad and Zack looked around for something that they could use to prompt against the wall.

Out of luck, Zack found two wooden solid crates from the left corner. It was their only chance to escape. Looking up from the window, Zack saw the solid ground.

Zack climbed up the crate and busted open the window with the metal pipe. "Yeah, we need to get out of here."

Devin shook his head and rubbed it until he got up from the floor. "They won't get far!"

Devin pulled out his remote control to turn off the lights in the hallway and the room, leaving Toad and Zack in complete darkness.

"Damn--The lights are out!" Zack said, "Come on, take my hand."

Zack held on to Toad's hand, pulling at the edge of the window. They both nodded and jumped off from the edge of a two-story building, landing on the ground. Loud barking was heard in the yard.

Zack looked up and saw five German Shepherd's upon them, surrounding them. One of the German Shepherds covered in blood growled at Toad a few inches from his face. It revealed all of its teeth.

Zack and Toad got up from the ground and their backs leaned against each other. Toad took up his knife and Zack tried to pick up the pipe in hand. German Shepherds barked from the right, threatening him. Its brown cold eyes glared at both of them.

When Zack reached for the metal pipe with speed, one of the dogs moved in and grabbed hold of his wrist. It clapped down hard, twisting its head right and left. "Get off my hand!" Toad took a knife and stabbed the dog in the torso twice. It yelped and let go. Zack winced from the pain of his bleeding wrist as he held it. The dogs growled in unison and barked, closing the distance between them.

Then, all of a sudden, a high beam flashed in the yard, a whistling sound was heard from a distance. "Sit!" Devin commanded. All of the German Shepherds obeyed. One of them whined.

Devin noticed his dead dog on the ground bleeding out blood and whimpered for the last time. He held his ax close to his shoulder. Devin's golden Mask shone against the moonlight. His eyes honed in on Zack and Toad like a heat-seeking missile ready to detonate.

"There is nowhere to run," Devin said as the dogs growled in the background.

"Time to play," Devin said. "That is if they survive my latest traps."

"Come on Zack let's run," Toad said.

Toad and Zack ran into the woods. The dogs were barking loudly and growling. "Let's give them boys a five-minute head start."

Zack and Toad kept on running. All the blood, pumping through their legs and arms. Each breath they took became shallow. Survival was what mattered. Getting as far away from Devin and his crazed dogs was their key to survival. Perspiration was instant throughout their clothes as they were running so hard. Each breath they took became shallow. Their legs pounding on the saturated ground of brown dirt as if they were on a sprint. The further they ran, the more lost they became.

"Come on, Zack, try to keep up!" Toad said.

"I am right behind you," Zack said, pumping his legs and arms harder.

"Our only chance to get out of here is to find help," Toad said, breathing hard.

Underneath Zack's foot, a metal bear trap caught his ankle as he went down on the dirt face first. "Ahh!"

Toad stopped and turned around. "Zack!"

"Oh, God! It hurts!" Zack yelled.

"Hold on, Zack! I will get this off you," Toad said.

Toad took the metal bar and pried it against the teeth of the bear trap. He pushed harder against it with all of his strength. Zack moved his foot out of the bear trap. Moments later, Devin whistled, commanding his German Shepherds to go after them. Their barking startled Zack and Toad. Toad pulled up Zack from his arms and held him by the shoulders.

"Zack, look down there!" Toad said.

"I don't believe it," Zack said.

They saw flashing red and blue lights and the word "Police" written on the side door.

Zack and Toad slid down the hill and approached the police car of a man sitting on the driver's side. The dogs barking got louder and louder.

"Officer, I'm so glad you are here," Toad said. "There's a crazy psycho in a mask with dogs trying to kill us. Officer? Officer?" He touched the policeman on the arm as the officer's face fell limp to the side with his mouth parted with a slit throat. His eyes, missing from his sockets.

Zack opened the door and noticed by luck that the key was still in the ignition."Toad, I need your help to get his body out of the car." Toad helped Zack heave the officer's body off the seat and planted him on the ground. Toad took the officer's handgun attached to his belt. He lifted it off from the dark holster. Four dogs appeared barking loudly.

"Get in the car!" Toad said starting the car and rolling up the power window. One dog collided against the glass. Barking and face on the glass.

Another German Shepherd jumped on the front hood with its front paws on the car. Its eyes narrowed, with sharp teeth. It growled eagerly to tear them apart.

"Toad, do you know how to drive?" Zack asked.

"Hell yeah! I just got my permit," Toad said.

Devin from the shadows leered forward with his ax at the roof of the police car. Toad and Zack screamed. Devin swung the ax again, driving the tip of the blade deep into the hood.

Toad put the car in reverse and then put his foot on the brake, forcing Devin off the hood. He shifted the gear to drive and mashed down on the accelerator. Toad swerved to the side, forcing the dog off the front hood.

"I hate these dogs," Toad said.

"Me too!" Zack said, sighing for relief. His ankle ached from the bear trap.

Toad got on the main road, watching his side-view mirror. "I got a plan. We head to the police station and tell them what happened."

"Well, we are safe!" Zack said, "I thought we would be a goner in that place."

"No, I wasn't going to let that happen. I always got you back, "Toad said.

Toad saw a high beam of light flashed from a car behind him. The car sped up and hit the back bumper. Toad looked at the mirror again when he realized it was Devin, driving a black Dodge to a pickup truck. He pulled up from the side and rammed against the police car, pushing them toward the railing. Toad tried to put distance from Devin.

"Leave us alone!" Toad shouted.

With quick thinking, Zack took the safety off the gun he took from the policeman. He pressed on the power window button in order to roll down the window from the passenger side and leaned out firing shots at the tires. One of the bullets ricocheted off the side of the truck. A second bullet hit the front tire of Devin's truck, causing it to skid off the side of the road.

"How did you learn how to shoot like that?" Toad asked.

"My father taught me when I was ten," Zack said.

They both looked at each other and started laughing.

Devin had beaten his hand against the steering wheel. Then, his brain clicked. He realized that his prey would head to the police station. The same police station he destroyed. A cold smirk had risen from his face as the sky rumbled with thunder and lightning soon followed.

Chapter 11

R obert arrived at the safe house from Lake Len Avenue, which was fifteen miles north from home. He pulled up his red Jaguar on the gravel, parked it, dimming the lights and turning off the ignition with his key. Robert's head still throbbed as he reached in his pants pocket for a pain pill to relieve the massive headache. He took one pill and swallowed it while chasing it down with his bottled water that was kept close to the cup holder. The refreshing liquid kept his body cool. He neglected the fact to seek medical intervention. Then again, he had experienced worse.

Jennifer woke up yawning and opening her eyes. "I will take it we are here."

"We are here," Robert said, glancing at her, unbuckling the seat belt, and opening up the door to get out.

"Mommy!" Kevin said, wiping the crust from his eyes with his hands.

Jennifer opened the back door and unbuckled his seat belt. "Yes, baby?"

"Where are we, mommy?" Kevin asked. "I want to go home."

"We are at a private house that your grandpa picked for us to stay at for a little while," Jennifer said, rubbing his head. "Don't worry, we will go home when it's okay."

"I can't believe Kevin is six," Robert said, picking up her bags.

"He turns seven next week," Jennifer said.

"Where is Daddy!" Kevin asked as if looking for answers.

Robert and Jennifer looked at each other, knowing that they can't say what happened to him, protecting his fragile heart. They both look at Kevin, not acknowledging he has been kidnapped.

Robert smiled. "Hey, kiddo, I know you miss your daddy. "But I promise. I will bring him home to you. I just need you and mommy to stay in this house for now. If you're good, I can go out to the store later and get you some ice cream."

Kevin's eyes bulged in excitement. "Ice cream!"

"Yeah, what kind do you like?"

"Umm, chocolate chip cookie dough ice cream," Kevin said.

"Alright, I will get you chocolate chip cookie dough ice cream! The best kind," Robert said with a warm smile.

Robert averted his eyes when he noticed a familiar face, waiting for him at the parking lot space. "Hey, Robert, I see you all made it."

"Kenny, good to see you," Robert said. "Do you mind giving me a hand with this bag?"

"Yeah, let me take that off your shoulders," Kenny said.

Kenny took Robert's bag and rested on his shoulders. "What do you have in this bag lead? Cast iron?"

Kenny, this is Jennifer and my grandson Kevin," Robert said.

"Hi, nice to meet you," Kenny said, extending his hand. "Robert told me about you."

Jennifer shook his hand, staring at his ripped muscles from his chest and broad shoulders. "Likewise."

Kenny led Robert, Jennifer, and Kevin to a thick brick grey fortress. Going through the front doors, Robert was astonished to see how everything looked inside. The amount of work and money put into creating such a place. From the extravagant furniture to the kitchen to the dining room. It was equivalent to living with the rich and wealthy. State of the art cameras were in place. From the likes, no one had seen before.

The same for the motion detection sensors that were scattered outside in different areas of the house. Seven flat screens TV's monitors that were mounted in places across the house to see who comes within two feet of the house. Jennifer had never been into a home like this. For a moment, she felt safe. Kevin's feet were heard across the halls, reminiscing through the hardwood floor. He ran around the house, exploring around the floor, laughing at himself.

Robert was able to put down Jennifer's and his bags in the bedroom on the first floor on the side of the bed. He took a second to catch his breath, eyeing the queen size bed in front. "I'm getting too old for this." Robert stretched his back.

Kenny walked into the room with a traveling bag and placed it next to Robert's. "So, on a scale between one and ten? Ten being your worst, how do you feel, Robert?"

"To be honest, I feel like crap," Robert said.

Kenny chuckled. "I'm glad you are still alive."

"Me too! Have you heard anything about Captain Cambell?" Robert asked.

"Come to think of it, Aran and I had been searching for her. She is still missing. You don't think the Masked killer?"

"That is a possibility, but I'm not ruling it out," Robert said.

"I haven't seen Justin in a while. Is he alright?" Robert asked.

"No, he hasn't been the same since that bastard butchered Gabriel. He was over at the old police station for days, searching for clues that would lead him to find that psychopath. The man hasn't slept in days."

"I don't blame him," Robert said. "Losing a friend and partner is hard."

Kenny's cell phone vibrated in his pants. "Excuse me," Kenny said, answering the phone and putting it to his head. "Hello."

"Dad!"

"Zack, is that you? Where are you?"

"I'm at the police station with Toad. Some crazy guy in a golden mask; he is trying to kill us!"

"Okay, Zack, I need you to stay calm. I will be right there," Kenny said.

"I think he is here!" Zack said. "Please hurry, Dad!"

"I'll be right there," Kenny said. "Remember what I taught you."

Zack ended his call. Robert recognized the look on Kenny's face. The look of a worried parent for his child.

"Hey, is everything alright?" Robert asked, searching through his eyes.

"Yeah, my son Zack is having trouble with friends. He wants me to go over and pick him up," Kenny said.

"Do you need a hand?" Robert asked.

"I am okay. Make yourself at home with your family. I will be right back," Kenny said.

Robert knew Kenny was hiding something and was only telling him what he wanted to hear. Kenny left the room. He went through the front door toward his car.

"Kevin!" Jennifer yelled, calling out to him. "You can't be running around in the house."

"Oh, come on, mom! "Kevin said, scoffing at her voice while sucking his teeth in frustration. "You can't be running around in the house," Kevin repeated, mocking her tone.

Robert was right behind him smiling. He thought about Jordan in how he would repeat the same behavior toward his mother whenever he would do something out of character. Whether it would be Jordan, forcing his aunt to sit in the back seat of the car while sitting next to his mother, or hogging the DVD player from the living room, so he can watch his cartoons. Robert missed the innocence of Jordan that he sees in Kevin. But Kevin was different. He was shy, yet curious. A lot like Robert.

"Kevin, do you want some Sloppy Joes? I know how much you like to eat them."

"Yeah, Papa," Kevin said, taking Robert's hand.

Robert walked with Kevin toward Jennifer in the kitchen. The smell of Sloppy Joe filtered the air. Kevin went to his seat by the table eager for it.

"Umm, that smells good, Mommy," Kevin said.

"Don't worry the food will be ready in a minute," Jennifer said, stirring sloppy Joe with a wooden spoon.

"Hey, Jennifer, I am gonna go and follow Kenny. I think he is in trouble. If by any means, I don't return, call Aran. The number is on the table counter. He will look after you too!"

"Robert, be careful," Jennifer said.

"I will be careful. Hey, kiddo I will be right back. I need to run to the store and I will bring you back something," Robert said.

"Okay, Papa, I love you," Kevin said.

"I love you too, Kiddo," Robert hugged and kissed his forehead.

* * *

Thirty minutes had passed. Zack and Toad were hiding from Devin at the police station. He waited in his car, revving up the engine, clapping down on the steering wheel of his black Mustang. He looked upon the night sky, pulling out a set of knives from a black porch. He touched the blade with his gloved hands, breathing heavy. Devin pulled up his car around the corner with his high beams on. He saw the police car abandon.

"I know they are here," Devin said, reviving his engine again, releasing exhaust.

"Toad we got to get the move on!" Zack said.

"I'm coming," Toad said.

Zack climbed quickly over the fence that would lead directly to the junkyard next to the police station. He waited for Toad to catch up.

Toad struggled to climb up the fence. His arm hurt from the previous attack from Devin. "Come on, Toad, you're almost over--"

Devin's car pulled up around the corner, eyeing both Zack and Toad by the fence. He waited for them to make their move. His heart pounded in excitement. Devin's foot smashed down on the accelerator of the black Mustang, charging at them at full speed. Zack panicked and yelled at Toad to move out the way. Out of nowhere, a car from the side hit Devin's car, which caused his car to spin out of control, hitting against the wall.

A man stepped out of his car with his Glock in hand. "Zack!"

"Dad?" Zack asked.

"Yeah, stay over there," Kenny said, walking slowly to Devin's car.

Devin sneaked up behind him with his knives about to stab him in the back. "Dad, look out!"

Kenny turned in time, avoiding Devin's knife slashes. He swayed left to right as he fired his gun at Devin's right arm. Devin flinched back.

"That's for stabbing me!" Kenny said, firing another shot at Devin. Devin dodged and threw a knife into Kenny's arm. He moaned in pain. Kenny took it out and got it into a fighting stance with Devin, throwing down the gun to the side.

Devin took his second and blade and mirrored his movements. "Finally, someone who speaks my language! This time, I will make sure you are dead and then I will take care of those two teenagers. You will suffer for hurting me for the last time."

"Zack, get to safety!" Kenny said.

"No, we can't leave you!" Zack said.

"Do as I say! Go now!" Kenny said.

"Don't worry, it won't be long," Devin said.

Kenny and Devin clashed with their knives. They both were countering each other. Devin didn't realize that Kenny's specialty in knife combat was his greatest skill. This was based on his past training from the army.

Zack and Toad kept on running further in the junkyard. It was until Zack ran into someone and squirmed and shrieked against his touch.

"It's okay, you are safe," Robert said.

"It's my dad. He needs help!" Zack said.

"Okay, I want you two to head to my car and lock the doors," Robert said.

Robert ran to find Kenny with his gun in one hand and a flashlight on the other hand. He reached the fence and noticed it was locked by the chains. He fired two shots at the chains, freeing the fence. From the top of the hill, Robert so Kenny and Devin square off with their knives. Each bloody from knife wounds.

"Freeze! Hands up!" Robert shouted, holding a gun inches away from Devin's temple. "Drop the knife and kick it to the side! Do it!"

Devin dropped his knife with his hands up and kicked it to the right side of the ground.

"Well, well Detective Robert Maxwell!" Devin said. "We meet face to face!"

"Where are Jordan and Amber? Answer me!" Robert Commanded.

"Robert? You followed me!" Kenny said in shock.

"Yeah, I'm glad I did. I knew something was up when you left," Robert said.

"Oh, how touching!" Devin said. "It looks like I will get a two for one deal."

"I will ask again? Where's Jordan and Amber?" Robert asked.

Devin laughed in amusement. "If you kill me, you will never know where to find them."

Chapter 12

"Family is everything to a person. Is that right, Detective Maxwell. The moment we spend with our loved ones is what connects us. It's what makes us, how would you say, whole! You can easily tell from their eyes. The way they look upon you. How does it feel that I have the one thing that matters to you most?" Devin asked in a taunting tone.

"Where is Jordan and Amber? Where are they?" Robert demanded, stewing in anger, wanting to kill him with his gun.

"You have to play by the rules of the game, detective, in order to find your precious boy and Amber," Devin said.

"I want my son!" Robert said. "Where is Amber?"

"All you have to do is play another game with me and I will take you to them," Devin said.

"Don't listen to him. He is trying to play you," Kenny said. "Look, we can book his ass and interrogate him until the cows come home."

"Are you willing to sacrifice your life for your boy? Amber? What's wrong Detective Maxwell? Cat got your tongue?"

"Shut your fucking mouth!" Robert said. "I had enough of your games!"

"You know your wife Amber has beautiful skin and her hair smells like peach-mango. Oh, I have been spending quality time with her in my private room. We had much to talk about."

Robert's hands were poised on the gun. He was tempted to shoot Devin in the back of the head.

"I wonder why she doesn't talk about you much? Was it because you have been banging that blonde hair girl for two years while married to Amber. Rachel was her name. Whatever happened to her?" Devin asked.

Kenny looked at Robert in a confused stare.

Devin turned his head to Kenny. "Oh, you didn't know. I wouldn't be surprised. With all that pillow talk he does with his mistress on the side. Your friend here has a lot of secrets buried in his closet. Isn't that right, Detective Maxwell?"

"What the hell are you talking about?" Robert asked. "What do you want from me?"

"This is the problem I have. No one takes the time to reflect on their past actions. They just react. I think it is high time for you to reflect, Detective Maxwell. For what you did twenty-five years ago, for what you did to RJ! I think you are ready for your trials."

"What trials?" Robert asked. He bit his lip in anger.

"You will face five trials Detective, Maxwell. It will be a test that you will never forget."

"And, if I refuse to participate?"

"If you don't play my game, there will be consequences. Your son Jordan will be the first to die. And then, after I am done with Amber, I will send you the best parts of her. You have my promise on that."

Robert was conflicted with two choices. Either go along with the trial or risk losing Jordan and Amber. His eyebrows arched into a frown. His hands tightened with rage.

"Time is ticking, the detective, I suggest you act quickly!" Devin said.

"Don't listen to this asshole!" Kenny said.

"You don't have that much time Detective Maxwell," Devin said. "It is now or never!"

Robert felt a steel gun pointed at his head." Drop the gun, Robert!"

Robert raised his hands up.

"Right on time!" Devin said, smirking under his golden mask.

"Justin!" Kenny said.

Justin Henderson showing up out of nowhere surprised both Robert and Kenny. They were both taken off guard.

Justin kicked Robert's gun away. "I'm sorry, Robert, he has my daughter. I had to follow the rules," Justin said in a distraught voice. "He told me if I didn't help him, she would die. The Mannequin killer wrapped her body in chains on a chair with a C4 bomb strapped to her chest. I have less than an hour to play his game. I know you would do the same thing in my position."

"Justin, you don't have to do this!" Kenny said with hands up.

"Don't move, Kenny! I don't want to shoot you, but I will," Justin said. "I will blow your brains out, you hear me! Don't take another step."

"Listen, Justin, you don't have to play his game. We can figure this out. We are on the same side here," Robert said.

"If you don't play the game, there will be consequences, Mr. Henderson, the dead man switch attached to my palm can be pressed." Devin showed Justin a flat metal plate, covering his palm with a small red button in the center. "If you don't do as I say. In one hour, I will press the button and Casey will explode into a thousand pieces. If either of you tries to kill me, the trigger to the bomb will go off the moment my heart stops beating. All that will be left of Casey will be a pile of guts and blood."

"My baby girl, Casey! She is only eighteen years old. I watched her graduate from high school and she was planning on attending Redwood College in the Spring. She wanted to go for her Bachelor's degree in Physical Therapy. All she ever wanted to do was help people, to make a difference. I can't lose her Robert. I just can't lose my Casey," Justin said.

"Take Detective Maxwell to your car," Devin said, holding his hand in place to press on the button.

Justin glared back at Devin with fear in his eyes, thinking about his daughter's life on the line.

"Do it, or she dies!" Devin said. "It's your choice!"

"Justin, I understand your pain," Robert said. That bastard has Jordan and Amber. We can figure this out!"

Justin pushed Robert to walk. "No, you can't! "Kenny, don't follow us. I will shoot you. I mean it!"

Justin led Robert to his white 2020 Toyota Camry. He popped open the hood of the truck with his key fob. Kenny stood still not moving since Justin kept his eye on him. "I mean it, Kenny doesn't follow me!"

"Get in the truck!" Justin said, pushing the gun on Robert's back, looking back at Kenny. "Get in now!"

Robert got in the trunk. Justin closed it.

"Give me the fob!" Devin said.

Justin gave Devin the key fob. He took it from Justin's hand. "What about my daughter Casey? We had a deal! I gave you Robert for the exchange of my daughter's life."

Justin's face expressed a moment of relief as he was breathing hard. "But, I never said you were off the hook." A small knife slid from Devin's dark sleeve sweater from his hand. Before Justin reacted, Devin took the knife and slit his throat with a deep slash at his neck.

Blood gushed out from the jugular vein as Justin held on to his wound from the neck. Thick blood seeped through his fingers and hand. He went down, dropping the gun. Devin drove off in his car. Kenny ran to him and picked up Justin's gun and started firing at the car. The bullet grazed the back window with three bullet holes.

Justin, in a barely audio voice, called out to him. "Take care of my daughter Casey. Tell her that I--"

Justin died instantly in his arms, covered in blood. "No! don't you die on me? Justin! Justin! God, no!" Kenny said, breaking down holding on to Justin.

Jamie heard his father screams and his friend Toad followed behind.

Kenny looked up at Jamie with tears in his eyes. "Son, call the ambulance with the cell phone in the car."

"Dad is he?" Alright, I will call them," Jamie said.

* * *

Three hours later. Devin drove the car to an unknown remote location about 50 miles outside of the town of Redwood. It was a wooded area surrounded by trees. Robert, for the past hour, had tried to break out of the trunk to escape, but the emergency latch had been removed. Robert banged against the trunk door, swearing under his breath. The car stopped. Devin opened the car door and closed it. Robert heard hollow footsteps approaching.

"Detective Maxwell, I suggest you get some rest. You will need all your strength for the first trial," Devin said. "I placed food and water in the bag in the trunk with you, so you won't be hungry."

"Wait! You can't leave me here!" Robert yelled, banging his fist against the trunk door. "It's not over!"

"No, it is just the beginning!" Devin said. "You will see. I will keep in touch, detective! I will tell Jordan and Amber you send them your best!"

"When I get out of here, I'm gonna kill you with my bare fucking hands!" Robert shouted "Get back here! Let's finish this!"

Devin walked up to five men. These men were killers and former mercenaries. Each used different tactics in terms of hunting their prey. Devin promised them a good hunt with Robert Maxwell. If one of them wins in killing Robert, they would get their prize money of five million dollars as agreed.

"As you all are quite aware, I have set traps all over the woods to make this game interesting," Devin said. "Any questions?"

"So, when do we start!" One mercenary said who carried a backpack with a flamethrower gun attached with a grenade launcher.

"We start tomorrow at 2 pm. I will be watching you all through the cameras," Devin said. "Good night, gentlemen."

"This is it! This is what I've been waiting for, baby! I can't wait to use my special tools," a second mercenary said.

"He's my prey and mine alone!" The first mercenary said. "I get first dibs!"

The other three mercenaries talked among themselves, flipping coins on who will go after Robert in the second round.

"Heads, I win!" a third mercenary said. "Looking forward to the hunt. May the best man win!"

Devin got in his spare car and drove off. He turned his GPS on. He switched on the camera in his car and watched in two separate feeds of Jordan as his head was face down and Amber who was crying hysterically. His hand glided to Amber's image as he touched her image on the monitor with his fingers. He started the car and left the woods.

"Don't worry, Amber, I will keep you company!" Devin said.

Chapter 13

For the past five days, Sam has been at Charles's house. He has been quiet, sitting at the living room black leather couch, drinking chocolate hot cocoa from a red coffee mug with homemade baked chocolate chip cookies. There were small little marshmallows that floated on the top surface of his white mug. He glanced at them in amusement, moving his feet up and down.

"This is really good," Sam said, chewing and swallowing the chocolate chip cookie.

"If you want some more hot chocolate cocoa and chocolate chip cookies, you can let me know," Charles said.

"Okay," Sam said with a slight nod.

Sam, for the first time, felt safe in someone else's home. He was wearing a striped red and white shirt with a pair of blue jeans and white sneakers. He enjoyed his freshly clean clothes. Sam looked around the room and noticed picture frame portraits of Charles with a young boy and a woman. "Who are they?" Sam asked, pointing his finger at the picture from the right side of the corner.

"Oh, that is my wife Amanda and my son Matt," Charles said.

"She is pretty," Sam said. "Are they here?"

Charles smiled at Sam. "No, they are not here. They had passed away. Sam, you never told me how you ended up in my car. Were you running from someone?"

Sam sipped more of the delicious hot chocolate cocoa. He looked up to Charles and placed his mug on the table. "I had to get away from my uncle. He hurt me." Sam looked away in shame.

"Sam, how did he hurt you?" Charles asked, leaning down and putting his hand on Sam's shoulder for comfort.

"When he gets mad, he locks me in a room. I would be there for a long time alone," Sam explained. "If I do something bad, he will hurt me. All I do is play with cars. How is that bad?"

"No, that is not a bad thing at all," Charles said. "It is okay to play with toys you enjoy. No one should punish you for that."

Sam stood up and turned around. He lifted up his shirt from the back to show Charles the deep scars. That looked like burnt marks done by an iron used to flatten out the wrinkles in clothing.

"He did this to you?" Charles asked in shock.

Sam scoffed as his lips curled, holding back the tears. "Yeah, my uncle did this to me! I had to get away."

Charles reached his back to touch Sam's leather deep scarring that left iron mark streaks. Sam closed his eyes, feeling ashamed of what happened to him.

Charles rolled back down his shirt. Sam turned around and got up from the couch to hug Charles from the waist for comfort. He started to wail with tears that flowed down his cheeks.

"It's okay, Sam, you are safe here. I will take care of you. You are welcome to stay as long as you like. I will keep you safe."

Charles's home phone started to ring. "Excuse me, Sam I will be right back. I'll bring you some more chocolate chip cookies. In the meantime you're welcome to watch TV until I return." Charles handed him the remote from the table and walked out of the living to answer the phone.

The phone rang the fifth time as Charles walked to the counter. He answered the phone and held it to his ear. "Hello."

"Charles, how are you doing?"

"Kenny?"

"You were expecting someone else?" Hey, I need your help. I was wondering if Jamie can spend the night over at your house for like a week?"

"Is everything ok, Kenny?"

Kenny paused for a moment. "No, I don't think everything will be okay. I just need you to look after Zack for me. That would be a huge help."

"Okay, Zack is more than welcome to my home."

"Thank you, I owe you one. It's really bad out here. There is a serial killer who killed many feds and men in blue."

"The Mannequin Killer. Yeah, I have been following the news. The police uncovered twenty bodies at the Red Cedar Park last week. A lot of them were women. I feel for the families honestly. My heart goes out to them. I'll be here. You can stop by the house."

"Thank you, Charles! You are the best. When this is all over, I will treat you and Jamie out to the Woods Steakhouse. It would be my treat," Kenny said.

"What are neighbor's are for," Charles said. "I'm just returning the favor. You helped me out when I was in a dark place. It is the least I can do."

"Hey, I don't mean to be a pain in the ass," Kenny said. "But, how are you holding up? I know it has been two years since Amanda and Matt passed away."

"I'm okay, taking it day by day, Kenny. I miss them all the time," Charles replied.

"I know it is not easy since that horrific car accident. I pray for you all the time," Kenny said.

"Thank you, Kenny!"

"I appreciate it, Charles. I mean it. Ok, I should be swinging by your house in a half-hour," Kenny said.

"Alright, then Kenny. See you soon."

Charles ended the call and placed the phone back on the charger from the table. He walked back to the living room to check on Sam.

"Hey, Sam! Do you want some more cookies? Sam?" Charles asked, walking back to the living room.

As Charles walked to the living, he noticed Sam was not sitting on the couch. The lights went out in the room. Charles searched for

Sam going up the staircase. He walked through the hallway until he entered Sam's room.

Charles opened the door to his room only to discover his bed was empty and unmade. He walked in panic and worry written on his face. Charles noticed the light from the lampshade was still on, resting from the top drawer.

The door was pushed to the side behind him, not closing completely without making a sound. Devin from the shadows, wearing his golden mask and a signature dark hoodie, stepped behind Charles. He held onto Charles's neck with one arm in a headlock. Climbing hard to cut off the airway. Charles struggled with each breath as his lips parted, desperate for air. He kept on elbowing Devin in the stomach, trying to put distance between himself and him.

A struggle ensued when Charles moved back against the wall, trying to shake off Devin. Devin took a needle out his pocket with his free hand. He popped off the top of a needle and stuck it into his neck, draining the contents into his vein. Charles went back against the wall again, knocking off the lamp off the top drawer. Charles's hands flung in protest. His eyes got heavy. In mere seconds, the strong sedative took him out cold.

"Nighty, night," Charles!" Devin said, dragging his body out of the room down the steps. "I have special plans for you."

Devin went down the steps with Charles's body. Charles's feet made heavy thuds on each step. "Almost there!"

Devin reached the bottom of the last step. He dragged his body out through the hallway, exiting the back door. Devin carefully checked his surroundings. He placed Charles's body in the trunk of his dark van and bound his feet and hands with a black twelve-inch cable zip tie and closed the trunk door. Devin got inside the driver seat and started the car. A young woman, who was a neighbor of Charles, spotted Devin and called the police. She hid around the corner near the side of her house, avoiding Devin's sight out of fear.

Devin looked over at Sam on the passenger side seat, checking to see if he was still out cold from the sedative. "Time to head home."

Devin drove off in a hurry. Not looking back.

"Hello, police! I would like to make a report. I just witnessed someone kidnap my neighbor," a young woman said.

Within five minutes, Kenny pulled up on a curve three blocks from Charles's house. The area was surrounded by five police cars. One policeman was interviewing the young lady who made the call.

"What the hell happened here?" Kenny asked, eyebrows arched. "Stay in the car, Zack," Kenny said. Zack looked through the window.

Kenny got out of the car and walked up toward Charles's home where a young woman was explaining details of a kidnapping. "Yes, I saw a man in a gold mask, black sweater, and blue jeans carrying Charles in the trunk of his car. He was at least six feet one inch."

"Can you describe the make or model of the vehicle?" One officer asked with a notepad and pen.

"Yeah, it was a dark van with tinted windows," the young woman said.

"Were you able to see the license plates?" The officer asked, eager to await her response.

"Actually, I took a photo of the license plate," a young woman said. "It's right on my phone." She showed the image to the police officer.

"Hey, what happened over here?" Kenny asked. "Where's Charles?"

"I'm sorry, but you can't come any closer," another officer said, putting his hand out to block Kenny from coming closer.

"I know you are doing your job. I'm a former cop. I know the gig. But I need to know? What happened to my neighbor Charles? Can you give me a straight answer, Officer Folder?" Kenny asked with arms out in the open, looking at his badge narrowing his eyes.

The officer glanced into Kenny's eyes for a while for recognition. The officer remembered seeing a photo of Kenny from the Redwood Police Department before it was destroyed in that horrific explosion. He turned around and glanced at the woman and the other police-men doing an investigation of the situation and then his attention returned back to Kenny. "Okay, from what I know? A suspect kid-napped a young male Caucasian, in his late thirties, with brown eyes and brown hair, wearing a plaid shirt with light brown khakis. He was last seen here." The officer pointed at the corner of the house. "That is all I can give you."

"Yeah, that sounds like Charles. Thanks!" Kenny said.

The police officer nodded. Kenny walked up to the young woman whom he recognized as Emily Smith. She saw Kenny, walking toward her direction. "Emily?"

"We will do what we can to find, Charles. You have my promise on that," the officer said. "Here is my card. Call me if you think you have anything else that comes to mind."

"I will Officer Murphy," Emily said, taking the card.

After investigating Emily, Officer Murphy went inside the police car to run a match on the license plates through the database.

"Kenny is that you?" She asked, hugging him. Filling up on his broad shoulders and well-defined arms. "I'm so glad you are here. I was scared out of my wits." Kenny pulled back and she ruffled her hand into her brown hair with her fingers, trying to calm her nerves. "I can't believe that creep took Charles!"

"Did you get a good look at him?" Kenny asked, staring into her eyes.

"Yeah, the guy had a creepy golden mask with that black sweater with a hoodie. The guy gave off bad vibes just like you see in those horror flicks. I thought if he saw me, I would be dead on the spot. I was afraid." She said with terror in her eyes. Emily took out a cigarette and started to light one up with her silver lighter. "I just hope those cops find Charles. He didn't deserve this!"

"I know," Kenny said. "Hey, were you able to get anything on the guy beside a mask?" Emily pulled out her smartphone and showed an image of a license plate RSE2345.

"Thanks, this is really hopeful," Kenny said. "You take care of yourself. If you need anything, call me. You have my number, right?"

"Yeah, I do. It is the same number, right."

"Yes, it is," Kenny said with a smirk.

Emily blushed looking at his eyes. "Yeah, sure I'll give you a call some time." She flaunted her hair.

Emily waved, staring at Kenny's body admiring the view. "Bye Kenny."

"Bye Emily," Kenny said with a smile.

Kenny walked back to his car, got in, and started the ignition. Zack shook his head. "That girl is thirsty for you, Dad!"

"Well, I'm gonna need a bigger hose then," Kenny said.

"She is hot, Dad! You should hook up with her," Zack suggested. "Plus, she is single."

"Now, my own son is giving me dating advice. What is the world coming to?" Kenny said with a smirk.

"Come on, Dad? When was the last time you were happy?" Zack asked. "Be honest with me?"

"Since your mother," Kenny said with a low tone.

"I miss her too, Dad! But, I think she would want you to be happy. I do too."

Kenny thought long and hard on what Zack told him. "Maybe you're right, son, maybe I do deserve happiness. I'm gonna take you to someplace safe for the meantime."

"Where's that at?" Zack asked.

"Oh, you will see for yourself when we get there," Kenny said.

Chapter 14

It was a quarter to two in the afternoon. Robert was desperate to escape the trunk of the car. He didn't bother eating the food Devin left him, thinking it was poison. Robert removed his shoe and searched his sock from his right foot. He felt the impression of an object on the side of his foot, drawing it out to his range of sight. It was the handiest thing to carry in most survival emergencies. He knew that his red pocket safety knife would come to his aid. Even in dire circumstances.

Robert touched all around the flat patting of the trunk, looking for any impressions that he could exploit. On the edge, Robert made a small cut on the fabric in the end. A sudden sound of static got Robert's attention. He hid his pocket knife out of sight by folding his hand. A video monitor came on from the trunk of the car.

Devin stared at Robert with hollow eyes. There was an emptiness to them that spoke of death. "Good afternoon, Detective Maxwell! I hope you are ready for the big day. Today will be your first trial. This will be a test to see your will to survive. So, let us begin. Do you see the image of Captain Cambell? She is inside a glass cylinder, hung upside down in chains. There are two tubes connected to a large two hundred gallon tank of melted yellow wax. In the corner of the tank, you will find two valves that will turn counter-clockwise to release a stream of wax that will flow through the two tubes to full up the tank."

Robert interrupted. "Why are you doing this? Captain Cambell had nothing to do with this!"

From the screen Captain Cambell fidget in movement. She screamed at the top of her lungs. "No, I don't want to die!" She banged her hands on the side of the glass.

"Oh, you are wrong, Detective Maxwell. She and the rest of the police department have to pay for their sins. Sins that the police tried so hard to bury, but we both know the truth will find a way to surface. There is a white envelope on the left-hand side of the trunk. Inside of it, you will find a key to a box that would deactivate the hot wax going into Captain Cambell's cylinder that is located close to an old house. If you get there before the two-hour deadline, you might have a chance to save her." The trunk door opened. Robert was surprised that it opened on its own. "I suggest you start moving, Detective Maxwell. She would make a nice piece like the others."

Devin ended his transmission from the screen. Robert got out of the trunk and took a moment to stretch his legs after being crimped in there for some time. He looked around at his surroundings. Only to discover he was in some derelict wooden shed with one visible light hanging twenty feet from him.

As Robert started moving, he heard something behind him. He crunched down and moved around the car to keep himself invisible in the darkness. Robert turned around and saw a medium built man in a black helmet and dark leather clothing with a flamethrower.

The mercenary grimaced with his eyes bulged at Robert. He knew he had to put distance from himself and the flame-throwing psycho.

"It's barbecue time!" The mercenary said, firing his flamethrower at Robert.

Robert dodged and rolled out of the flames trajectory with grace. The wall was scorched with flames. Robert got back up and ran toward the opening. The mercenary fired his grenade launcher at Robert. The detonator rotated in mid-air and made contact with the wall, exploding five feet that propelled Robert forward. He coughed from the dust and his body ached and was dazed from the blast. He quickly got up and moved out of his site hiding in the shadows, blending in with the smoke.

"Whoa! I love this gun. I will enjoy burning you," the mercenary said, getting excited about the kill. "Extra crispy!"

The mercenary walked through the smoke, firing his flamethrower again against the floor, trying to fry him on the ground swaying his flamethrower side to side. Robert ran through the opening of the hallway and blended in the shadows against the corner between a large pillar and a wall. Robert armed himself with his pocket knife. He held his breath and picked up a rock in front of him. Robert watched and listened for the creaking noise of the mercenaries' footsteps.

In his rearview, Robert saw the flame throwing mercenary insight. His flamethrower gun pointed straight. The tip of the gun ignited a small flame. As he walked further, Robert kept still, anticipating the tempo of his movement. He walked out of the shadows behind the mercenary. His hand gripped the rock. Robert arched in position with the blade in the other hand. He stepped slowly with caution. In the instant, Robert stabbed him in the side of the neck, with his pocket knife as if instinct took over.

The mercenary went down, dropping his flame throwing gun. Robert got on top of him and bashed his face in with the rock. The mercenary held his hands up, his eyes bulged in shock. Robert pounced on his face like a meat tenderizer in a mad frenzy. The mercenary nose was smashed inward, his jaw broken, including his front teeth as Blood splattered all over Robert's clothes. Red crimson blood stained Robert's face. He took the flamethrower, a large knife with a dark sheath, and radio off the dead mercenary. Robert got back up and started moving. Time was pressing on him to find the deactivation device to save Captain Cambell. He kept low, leaning against the boarded wall. He heard the radio go off.

"Hey Travis, did you toast that cop yet?" Asked the caller. "Travis, are you there?"

Robert turned off the radio. He looked out through a window and saw flashlights, beaming in his direction. "Shit!" He ducked with his weapon and moved toward the stairway, leading up to the top. It didn't occur to him that other mercenaries would be pursuing him in the trials. His main focus was to find the device and deactivate it.

Robert opened the door with caution, leaving a small crack. He felt the cool air entering from the steps. Robert went through the door, entering some unknown room littered with garbage. Cabinets, papers, and drawers scattered across the area. The air smelled of dead rats. Robert held his hand against his nose. His eyes became irritated by the amount of mold on the walls and floor.

Old newspaper clipping surveyed both sides of the walls. He kept on moving, hoping to find the nearest exit. Robert checked the doors near him only to discover they were locked. He banged on one door out of frustration. He went through the hall further to find two grey double doors that were locked with chains. He tried to adjust the setting to the flamethrower by turning the dial to the grenade feature. The contraption was complex. "Come on!"

Robert heard a click from the flamethrower. He aimed at the grey doors and fired, blowing up the doors. "Yeah, this will do."

He ran through the smoke of the opening. He breathed hard with each stride. He kept on moving toward the light and not looking back. He went through another door and hid in the shadows between a table and wall away from his pursuers. Robert heard someone go through the doors.

"He got to be close by!" One mercenary said. The fucker killed Travis! He was a greedy bastard anyway."

"Served him right. Hey, that means that we have a shot of the prize money!" A second mercenary said. "If we get this cop, I will split the money. I get half and you get half. How does that sound?'

"Sounds good to me," One mercenary said. "He can't be far. Be ready!"

"Right," the second mercenary said, giving him the hand signal.

He changed the setting of the flamethrower back to the flame setting. He took a deep breath as footsteps were moving in his direction. He glanced for second and saw the two mercenaries gaining a foothold.

He closed his eyes and turned as he opened them, firing his flamethrower weapon on both of the mercenaries. Their weapons went off. Not hitting Robert. Their screams were high pitched as the flames consumed their flesh, burning every square inch of their bodies. Robert ran past them and kept on going, running through doors.

When Robert stepped on the wood panel on the floor, in front of him, two mechanical axes came crashing down from both sides. He leaped to the side just in time, avoiding the axes from cutting off his head. Robert looked back at the contraption. He held his breath not knowing if he was gonna be a goner.

Robert heard static coming from a flat fifty-two widescreen TV that was thirty-six inches above him. The image came into focus with Devin in his golden mask, staring at Robert intently.

Devin gave an applause. "Bravo, Detective Maxwell! You have survived your first trial. Well done! But the game is not over yet. You still have less than an hour and fifteen minutes to find the device to save Captain Cambell." Devin switched the screen on Captain Cambell, revealing the first batch of hot yellow wax slowly entering her container. She screamed like a banshee, pounding at the glass. "Let's see if you will survive this challenge"

Follow the clues that would lead to your next trial. There is a sequence of five numbers. You need to enter them in the right order before you use the key to turn off the device. I suggest you hurry! She doesn't have that much time. When the clock hits zero, her body will be molded into my perfect wax sculpture. Preserved fever. Time is ticking, detective!"

"What clues?" Robert demanded in anger. His lips contorted.

After years of working with Cambell, Robert wondered if what Devin said was true. What secrets had been buried? Did she know something about the killer?

Robert continued to walk through the empty corridors. He kept his guard up for anything. On the corner of his eye, he spotted a white envelope laying on a table display that read open in black letters. He carefully ripped the envelope open and pulled out a white card.

Robert turned and glanced at the card. Twenty-five. On the wall, he noticed blue numbers scribbled on the wall that ranged from odd to even numbers. "What the hell? The clues to the numbers have to be related to the sequence of numbers. "The number eleven is repeated throughout the wall. It has to be the second number."

Robert kept on walking until he reached another door. He took the stairs to the second floor. There was an orange arrow painted on the side of the wall, pointing straight. He looked left and right, walking slow. Adjacent from him was an open window. Cool air blew in his direction. Robert reached for another room that looked like a dollhouse. The walls harbored shelves of dolls painted with white faces missing eyes from their sockets.

There were three mannequins covered in yellow wax that looked lifelike. Their mouths exposed, their eyes missing. Robert searched around for clues around themselves. He picked up one doll and tossed it on the floor. He rummaged through all the dolls, looking for any clues on the other sequence of numbers. When Robert pulled one doll on a string, the door locked. Robert turned and noticed the middle of the floor opened up, displaying a flat monitor attached to a pole hoisting itself upward. The screen came on and Devin's image was revealed.

"It is time for your second trial, Detective Maxwell!" Devin said in a proud tone.

Chapter 15

I t had been three hours. Kenny had been calling Robert's cell phone and all he got was his voicemail that was full of messages. The possibility that the Masked killer had gotten a hold of his phone was probable in his mind. He cursed under his breath and ended the call. Kenny held on to hope that Robert was still alive. It was a gut instinct he followed.

"Dad? Where are you going?" Zack asked.

"I'm going out to check up on Someone," Kenny said. "I haven't heard from him in a while. You and Toad stay here at the safe house with Jennifer and Kevin. I should be back within an hour, Toad?"

"Yeah," Toad said, looking up at Kenny.

"I need you to do something for me," Kenny said. He hands him a gold key.

Toad took the key from Kenny. "What is this for?"

"That is key to the weapon's safety. I know you will look after Zack like a brother and protect Jennifer and her kid," Kenny said. "Inside are handguns. If you don't feel comfortable with a gun, there are some aluminum bats you can use instead.

"You know me, Mr. Roger. Zack and I will protect them," Toad said.

"Okay be careful, Dad. I love you," Zack said, hugging Kenny.

"I love you too!" Kenny replied. "If things get out of hand, you and Toad take Jennifer and Kevin to the safe room. That will give you added protection. It is just like we practiced."

"You got it, Mr. Rogers," Toad said with a confident tone.

Kenny went out through the front door. He closed it as the security system kicked in, securing the perimeter. He pressed on a keypad four-digit pin that opened the thick reinforced steel wall. The wall lifted up like a garage door with the same humming noise. It left a big opening for him to walk through. The door closed on its own. As he walked on the hard paved sidewalk to his car, Kenny looked around for any people or vehicles. The area was clear. His only train of thought was about finding any leads on the Masked serial killer.

Kenny got in his blue 2018 Ford Mustang and started it up. He glanced at the radio and pressed the button. All he heard was the local weather and other local news coverage. His foot was on the brake as he placed the car in reverse. Kenny turned his head, looking behind his view, grabbing hold of the top seat on the passenger, and reversed the car out of the driveway turning his wheel.

Kenny drove through the open road. His car roared like a fierce beast as he passed other cars and headlights. On the corner of his eye, he spotted a gas station since his tank was near empty. He pulled his car up at the Sun Side gas station near the number ten pump. The regular unleaded was marked two dollars and thirteen cents a gallon. His eyes lit up when he saw the price again at a second glance.

Kenny got out of his car, feeling the cold wind against his face. He zipped up his coat. Carbon dioxide escaped his breath as he exhaled. From his black wallet, he took out his debit card and keyed in his pin, selected unleaded, removed the gas pump from the tank while removing his gas cap to begin feeling up his gas tank, pulling the lever from his hand. Kenny watched the screen on how much he was putting in. There were cars ahead of him, feeling their cars up with gasoline.

After Kenny finished filling up the gas tank, he went inside the store. The bell dinged twice when he passed through the door. He walked all the way to the back near the beverage aisle. Kenny was deciding on what type of beer to buy.

There were five people at the front register, paying for different items that ranged from lottery tickets, beer, food, and cigarettes. One guy that had a black cap and green sweater were on the opposite aisle from Kenny. The guy was stacking up on five boxes of condoms like it was his last night on earth.

"Looks like someone is packing some heat," a voice said. "Either that or he's planning on having a marathon."

Kenny chuckled. "I suppose so." He glanced at the woman next to him.

"Oh, I didn't know you work here," Kenny said. He noticed her Sun Side logo print on her shirt.

She gave off a wiry smile. "Yeah, I just finished my shift. Working the full nine-hour job as a sales clerk."

"Sounds like a cozy job," Kenny teased.

She tried to contain her laughter. "Hey, I didn't get your name. My name is Claire." She extended her hand.

Kenny took her hand. "Kenny."

"So, what brings you here in the neck of the woods?" Claire inquired.

"Nothing, really just following some leads," Kenny said.

"Leads? Are you a cop, or something?" she asked.

"I used to be but now I'm retired," Kenny said. "Long story."

"Long story you say," Claire repeated.

"Just like I said," Kenny said with a smirk. "I better get going. It was nice talking to you, Claire."

"Likewise, take care," she said.

"You too!" Claire said.

She waves, biting her lower lip, staring at Kenny's body. Her heart was pumping hard like a drum. Her eyes fixed on Kenny's buff well-defined shoulders, biceps, and chest. Claire could barely breathe at the sight of him. Her face was cherry red. Every tempo of her body quaked. She gasped for air, looking at Kenny's lips, soaking up the fantasy of ravaging them with her own.

Kenny intercepted the front desk, checking out his items of beer and chips and mini power white donuts. The cashier clerk added all the items from his registry, punching in his keys. "That will be thirty-two dollars." The cashier placed all of Kenny's items in a white bag.

Kenny took out his black wallet, taking forty bucks and handing it over to the cashier clerk. "Here you go."

Kenny received his eight dollars. "Thanks."

Kenny walked out through the door, the bell went off with two loud dings. As he walked out, he felt the dampness from the pavement. He looked up at the sky and noticed the heavy dark clouds. Kenny heard the loud roar of thunder. He approached his car. He opened the door and placed his supplies at the bottom of the back seat. Kenny felt his phone vibrate. He pulled his cell phone out and looked at the message.

"Dad be safe!" Zack said.

Kenny smiled and replied back. "I'll be safe soon. Love you!"

Kenny slid his phone back into his pocket. As he did that, he turned around for a split second only to find out it was Claire. His heart skipped a beat as he gasped for air. "Sorry, I didn't mean to scare you like that."

"No worries. For a moment, I thought you were someone else," Kenny said, laughing it off.

"You forgot this. I think this fell out of your wallet," Claire said, handing him a young picture of Zack when he was two.

"Thank you," he takes the picture from her hand and puts it in his wallet.

"Is that your boy?" Claire asked.

"Yeah, that is my son Zack. He was two years old. Now, he is seventeen. Time does fly"

"I know what you mean. I have a sister. She just turned nineteen. They grow up so fast," Claire said. "Hey, I was wondering if you were free to go to the annual Spool Festival that is being held this Saturday. The food and drinks are free. You can bring your son too if you like. Before you decide, here is my number.

Kenny reached for his cell phone. Okay, what's your number?"

"651-243-5832," Claire replied. "You call me to let me know."

Kevin Smiled. "I will let you know, Claire. Thanks for returning my photo."

"You're welcome. You have a good night, Kevin."

"You too Claire," Kevin said.

Claire walked away. Kevin got into his car and drove off from the gas station. He got on the intersection, while the headlights were still green. He made a right turn, turning the wheel slightly with his right hand. He rolled down the window midway to feel the cold air on his face to keep alert. Kevin thought about Claire's offer to attend the festival. How nice it would be to escape his dilemma.

The fact that Robert was still missing and a serial killer is still at large, tormenting this county left a series of uncertainty. There was no telling what sick game he was planning. The only thing he prayed and hoped for was that Robert would somehow survive this and come up on top. Kevin turned his hand signal to turn left on the runway. He looked to his left to see his way clear. Cars were moving about 55 mph ahead of him. He noticed a tractor-trailer was speeding up behind on the left side.

He picked up on the speed, putting distance between him and the truck. Then, in the instant, Kevin made the left turns while it was clear. He passed by the speed sign that read 50 mph. He looked to his left and noticed State Troopers parked in the middle off the thruway, waiting to bust someone with a speeding ticket, DWI, suspended license, the works. But they had a job to do and Kenny knew that because he was once a State Trooper. How he was glad to make the switch to the police department and retire with a nice pension.

Kenny got a call from his cell phone that should be up on the front screen. He answered the call on the Bluetooth feature from his car.

"Hey, Kenny I got the information on the plates for you and did some deep digging on information that would prove to be useful. Are you on your way?" A voice said.

"Yeah, Virgil I will be there within fifteen minutes. Good work!" Kenny said with praise in his voice.

"Okay, I'll be here," Virgil said. "I got nothing else better to do than to play chess online against some people around the world to cure my boredom."

"Right, I don't know anything about chess," Kenny said.

"It's really not that hard once you understand the principles of openings, chess notation, middle games, and endgames," Virgil explained.

"Sounds complicated and I don't have the patience for it. I will see you at your house," Kenny said.

The call ended. Kevin felt that this was the break he was looking for, the lead that he needed. He would have within his grasp the information on the possible identity of the serial killer.

Chapter 16

"It is nice to see you, the real you Detective. You have the same killer instinct. The ruthlessness that lay buried deep in that cold demeanor, the same bloodlust in your eyes just like twenty-five years ago when your partner got butchered to death. My thought of you never waivered not one bit. You and I are alike. Two halves of a coin, two killers reborn. That would do anything to live. The irony of it all. Admit it to yourself, you enjoyed killing that man just as much as I enjoyed it."

"We are nothing alike!" Robert shouted. "I will find you. I will end you."

"I beg to differ, Detective Maxwell," Devin said. "You can't deny what you are. The only difference is that you are not honest with yourself. Amber doesn't know about your private discretions. You have a lot of blood on your hands, Detective Maxwell."

Robert grew silent. He looked intently at the flat screen monitor of Devin in his golden mask. The lights flashed on and off in the room. "It is time for your second trial, Detective Maxwell." On the right side of the shelf, a timer started. "You have one hour to find the device to deactivate with the key to save Captain Cambell's life. The device is located on the third floor. Somewhere in one of the rooms. All you have to do is follow the clues to find the right room."The screen image switched to Captain Cambell with the hot yellow wax mixed with rubber, pouring in small streams. Some of the liquid scolded her right shoulder, torso, and arms. Her screams were heard through the monitor.

"Captain Cambell will pay for her sins and she will make a great mannequin minus the eyes of course. Time is ticking Detective Maxwell I suggest you get a move on," Devin said. "Her life is in your hands."

"This isn't over!" Robert said, eyeing the monitor, moving toward the door.

The monitor turned off. Robert opened the door. Unbeknownst to him, two other mercenaries were in hot pursuit of him down the hall. He picked up on the footsteps and hid in the shadows. The door leading up to the third floor was six feet from him. Time was imminent. The mercenaries armed with their M16 weapons, checked each corner of the hall.

"He couldn't be far. I know he is here. You check the rooms," one mercenary said. "Keep your eyes open, this guy is no ordinary cop. He definitely has a set of skills to fry our people like that."

"I don't care who it is. I'm gonna kill him," the second mercenary said. "He won't get away this time. "He will suffer for killing Travis! I will skin his ass slowly with my knife one layer at a time starting with his face. Then, the moment he begs for death, I will cut his heart out and put it on a skillet."

"Keep your head in the game. I can't afford you to get clouded by your need for vengeance. I need you here. I need you to hold your shit together. Can you do that?" One mercenary asked.

"Yeah, the second mercenary responded. "I will. I was thinking after we off this guy you and I can go on a trip."

"Like where?"

"I was thinking about Hawaii? There are a lot of women there and I heard the food is great there. Plus, it will be rich with that prize money of five million dollars. You can't beat that."

"Hawaii? Can you think of somewhere else?" The first mercenary asked him while tapping his chest and signaling with his fingers.

"Go check the rooms," the one mercenary said.

The second mercenary nodded and left him.

The mercenaries had no idea about Robert's past. They had no idea that he once served in the military before he became a cop. He kept that a secret from others, including Jordan. One person knew the truth and that was Kenny. The same Kenny who helped him manage the trauma of his PTSD.

He had flashes of memories from the early years in service with the army. The blood and carnage were all coming back to him in a rush. One minute he was talking to his soldiers, making plans to infiltrate an underground base of militia extremists. The second minute, he watched in horror as his friends stepped forward on landmines that were stationed within eight feet within the ground. Each of the soldiers walked up front of him once their feet planted on a flat metal plate coiled trigger, hidden in the dirt. One by one, they blew up in front of him into a multitude of pieces. Their blood and guts splattered all over his body that froze in a slow frame of a picture, capturing details of an everlasting impression. He wiped his eyes of the blood so he could see. The very jaws of death, clinching close to his heart. The rampant need for vengeance cooed in the open air like a whisper.

Robert came too as he clenched his fist and noticed the mercenary back was turned. An opportunity he couldn't miss out. He moved stealthily in the shadows. He pulled the missionary back, gripping his neck with his arms folded around the mercenary's neck. Robert applied pressure, squeezing as much air as possible. As the mercenary tried to force him against the wall, Robert dragged him further away from the other missionary. The missionary struggled from Robert's grip, clenching his hands against his arms. In a matter of minutes, he was out like a light. Robert laid his body against the corner of the wall out of sight and took his gun.

"Hey, Paul, how do you feel about the Bahamas? I haven't been there before. I know the food is great and some strong alcohol. I say after we take care of the cop we head over there. Paul? Paul, are you there?"

He went in the corner of the hallway with the gun, checking his right and left the range of sight for the other mercenary. His eyes were laser-focused. He ducked down between three dusty wooden crates. The second mercenary stuck his head out in the hallway, looking around. As the second mercenary went back into the room, Robert waited a few minutes to get in position. He then walked into the dark dim room where the second mercenary was, not drawing attention to himself.

He aimed his gun at the head of the mercenaries that was fifteen feet from him. He took one last breath and fired, putting a hole into the mercenary's head with a clean shot. The mercenary went down with a loud dud. Robert strode over to the body of the first mercenary in the hallway and put a bullet to his head.

Twenty-five minutes had passed. Robert ran to the door, leading to the third floor. He made his way to the top floor. In the corner of his eye, there were three white envelopes taped on the wall that were labeled one, two, and three in black ink. Robert unraveled the first envelope, revealing the contents that read, "The key to your salvation is near." He opened the second envelope and it read, "follow the patterns close to your heart." He opened the third white envelope and it read, " follow the black arrows on the wall."

Robert looked around the wall and noticed the black arrows painted on the wall. He thought about the clue from the second letter. "Follow the patterns close to your heart." What was close to his heart? He thought to himself. The first thought that came to mind was Jordan. He looked up at the wall again and noticed one black arrow with a crooked point that pointed north. Robert went into the arrow's direction that led him to a door on the far right. He turned the golden knob on the door and opened it. His eyes glanced at the metal contraption laid out in front of him. The paper and trash littered the room. Mice scattered at the sound of Robert's footsteps. Dust filled the air as he walked up to it seeing the towering grey device. A monitor screen flipped on at the center, seeing Devin in his golden mask with a dark hood.

Devin clapped his hand twice. "You passed your second trial Detective Maxwell. I admire your tenacity. I truly do."

Robert glanced at him. His gun, aiming for the monitor. "Just let her go and we can end this face to face!"

"There are three key entries. One of them is the entry to deactivate the device to save Captain Cambell's life. If you choose the wrong one, the hot wax will increase from the tank, consuming her entire lovely body like a hot fudge sundae. She will be my next display for the latest masterpiece. If you choose the second key entry, she will be electrocuted with two hundred milliamps of electricity since there are coils attached to her feet. I suggest you choose wisely. You have less than thirty minutes to decide. I will be taking good care of Jordan and Amber. I might even start sending pieces of Jordan to you in a couple of days. Then, when I'm done with him, I will have fun with Amber." Devin chuckled. "All to myself!"

"Don't you fuckin touch them, if you do, you're dead. Do you fucking hear me? I will kill you!" Robert said with intensity in his voice.

"Have fun Detective Maxwell!" Devin said waving bye, ending the video message.

"I will find you!" Robert shouted.

The image from the monitor came back on. Only it was showing Captain Cambell's screams as she kept her arms and hands close to her body to avoid the harsh burn of the hot wax and rubber.

Time was ticking with twenty minutes left, Robert had to decide which key slot to use. He had to choose from the other two slots to disabled the elaborate death trap to save Captain Cambell's life. But he knew if he messed up, she was as good as dead. Sweat perspired on his face. He didn't know which key slot to choose. He closed his eyes for a split second, hearing the clicking noise of the timer as it was counting down to zero.

Each second counts. Robert had to choose fast as the wax and rubber were gaining traction in her cylinder container. Then he had a thought. Follow the pattern close to your heart. Devin gave him the clue to choose the right key slot. "The middle one. It had to be it." Robert had the key and pushed it down into the slot. Five minutes was all that was left. He breathed hard, praying it was the right one. His left hand clenched into a fist. Sweat, pouring down his face in droplets. He wiped his face, eyeing the timer with two minutes to spare.

"Here goes!" Robert said. He turned the key.

Chapter 17

Robert held his breath, his jaw clenched, hoping he selected the right key slot to shut off the device. He looked up at the monitor and gasped at the fact the timer stopped at two seconds. The light from the device blinked once and became a solid green. He laughed, brushing off the anxiety. He knew Captain Cambell was safe and the hot yellow wax mixed with rubber ceased in disbursement.

The monitor switched back to Devin. He looked at Robert with his cold brown eyes under that golden Mask. "Well, done Detective Maxwell! You selected the right key slot to save Captain Cambell's life." The sound of the door clicked. "Now we will start with your third trial."

"Enough with your fucking games!" Robert said.

The monitor screen went dark, leaving static sound. Robert walked toward the green door lit by a red light bulb above it. He had his gun ready as he opened the door slowly. Robert walked forward until he came into contact with a dark curtain. The smell of rubber and hot wax was in the air. He pulled it back to discover a black polished wooden floor that looked like a stage on Broadway in a local Redwood, Washington theater. There were heavy stage lights that shined bright above him.

Robert glanced to his right and saw red chairs in three rows. All of which contained one hundred mannequins. Fifty-two victims were among them that Devin had killed. They were all well preserved to be his special project. He wanted to show a display as a work of art. Each of the victims was well-dressed men and women. Devin admired his accomplishment. Rattling Robert to the core, testing the limits.

The putrid smell of formaldehyde alone forced Robert to cover his nose. He looked up and noticed a glass cylinder that contained Captain Cambell, hanging fifteen feet upside down in mid-air by chains on two large distinct dark pulleys attached to the ceiling. To Robert's eye, it resembled a coffin. He pointed his gun around to make sure no one else was around to catch him off guard.

"Help! Help!" Captain Kate Cambell screamed and rattled with fear as she banged against the glass. Her hand poised from exhaustion.

"Don't worry, Captain I'm gonna get you down," Robert said, touching her shoulder.

Robert searched all around. He spotted the chains. He ran toward them and yanked them down, causing the cylinder to move in a downward direction. "Just hold on Captain!"

The moment the cylinder hit the floor. Robert looked for any object he can use to smash against the glass cylinder open. He picked up a long metal pipe that was on the corner. "Cover your eyes," Kate covered her face with her hands as Robert banged against the glass until it went into pieces. Each shard fell against her skin down inside the contraption. He leaned in and grabbed Captain Campell out of the cylinder. She hugged him, tears ran down her face. For the first time in her life, she felt vulnerable. Her legs were shaking.

"It's okay, Kate!" Robert said, reassuring her. "Come on, let's get the hell out of here. Can you walk?"

Kate nodded her head. Her eyes spoke only fear and uncertainty.

"Good, come with me, "Robert said, holding her fidget hand. "Don't worry, I won't let that crazy son of a bitch get you. We are gonna come out of this alive."

Hearing those words breathe a sense of comfort compared to the confines of being inside that container, knowing her final moments were upon her. "Do you know a way out?"

"Yeah, I have some ideas. Let's just hope our ride is still there," Robert said. "We better get me moving to escape this psycho and the fucking trials."

"What trials?" Kate asked in confusion.

"Trust me you don't want to know," Robert explained.

"Right, I will follow your lead," Kate said.

Robert and Kate went through the green door, leaving the bodies of Devin's twisted fantasy room of death. Robert had to come up with a plan to escape together from the dusty labyrinth. The first thought that came into mind was to return to the very car he was placed in. All they had to do was to hotwire it and they would be home free.

***

A round camera feed from the top wall captured Robert and Captain leaving the stage. Devin watched Robert's heroics. His fingers folded on the hilt of his favorite blade as his nostrils flared with brown eyes, blinking at the monitor from his private darkroom. He began to breathe heavily, touching the monitor, gliding his fingers across the screen." Cambell, Cambell you think you are free? Nobody can escape me. Not even you Detective Maxwell. Your next trial will come. Just wait and see!" Devin plunged his favorite knife into the table with a strong force. He fantasized about what he would do with her. Then, Devin heard Amber woke up from the other monitor and left his room.

Another man from the corner approached him and pushed him against the wall. He stared at him intently with cold brown eyes. He wore the same black sweater and blue jeans. "You need to kill that cop. He needs to die for what he did to our father!"

"Robert Maxwell will be dead, Martin, once he passes the fifth trial. You can bet on that brother."

"Cambell we will deal at a later time, but our agenda is with Robert and Kenny," Devin said with conviction.

"Good, I got a score to settle with that friend of his friend Kenny Rogers," Martin said. "Since he shot me twice. This time he will die by my blade.

"That's what you get for pretending to be me," Devin said, mocking him.

Martin punched Devin in the jaw. Devin licked his bloody lip. Martin grabbed him by the collar with both hands.

"We made a promise together! "Martin snapped.

"I know and I won't break it," Devin replied, pushing his hands off him. He punched Martin with a right hook. "You hit like a bitch! Even the father hit harder than that."Martin clenched jaw while rubbing it.

Martin was Devin's identical twin brother. It was difficult to tell them apart from their dashing good looks. He was more tech-savvy compared to his brother Martin. Where he was more hands-on. Martin has proved himself, since day one, that he was worthy of their cause to have Robert Maxwell eliminated. Martin sensed and intercepted what his brother was thinking. They did everything from their first kill of their science teacher in twelfth grade which resulted in a botched lab experiment. Devin and Martin's bond was as strong as cast iron. Martin aided him to torment Robert Maxwell and killed Gabriel and the rest of the police force with the air drones he aided in creating. Just like Devin Martin wanted nothing more to make Robert suffer for what he did to their father twenty-five years ago.

"Tell me you are not seeing that woman again," Martin asked, looking into his eyes."

"Why? Are you jealous Martin?" I see the way you look at her."

Martin grew quiet and turned his eyes away.

"We share everything, there are no secrets between us," Devin said. "I know your intentions. Your desires," Devin said.

"She needs to go," Martin said to his face. Then, you know how I feel about her."

"No," Devin protested, "She lives! "Amber is mine and no harm will come to her."

"Can't you see she is poisoning your mind," Martin said. "She needs to die!"

Devin hissed and ignored that request. "You are wrong Martin and I will prove it to you."

"Don't you walk away from me," Martin said, grabbing Devin's arm.

Devin looked down at Martin's hand on his arms.

"Why do you waste your time with this woman?" She is not a family. Sam is our family. Have you forgotten that? You made a promise to Jeff, our brother, that you would take care of him even when cancer consumed him."

Devin flinched off Martin's grip from him and reached for his face with bulged eyes. "Because I like this one. Now, if you excuse me. I don't want to keep her waiting. I didn't forget Jeff's promise."

Martin frowned with heavy disapproval and his arms folded. Knowing full well he will have to take matters in his own hands. "You are blind brother, but I will fix that. Once that woman is out of the picture."

Devin walked five blocks from the hallway and opened the door to her cell. As he opened the cell, he smelled her malodorous body.

Amber's black hair and clothing disheveled. Devin's eyes were livid with deep hatred that he took a water hose attached to the wall six feet from where he stood, turned on the valve, and sprayed her down with cold water. Amber's hands flinch, trying to block the force of the water coming at her. Devin believed in cleanliness and his OCD went into hyperdrive. Everything had to be perfect. If there were any disorder in his environment, he would snap.

"Please, no more!" Amber yelled as her hands blocked a wave of water from her face.

"No, I can't have you being dirty," Devin said, directing the hose at her body and face.

Devin stops and reaches for a top-shelf full of white towels. He leaned down and placed the towel against her shivering body. "I got some fresh clothes for you to change into. If you behave yourself, I can take you to a warm shower. I know you must be starving. I made beef stew. I hope you don't mind."

"Please, just let me go!" Amber said, crying with tears, shivering from her cold damp clothes. Water drops dripped from her drenched clothes.

Devin turned off the valve from the hose and placed it down on the floor. He touched her shivering face and hair. "No, I can't do that. If it's any constellation, I see so much potential in you. You are a beautiful woman Amber. I can see why Robert took a liking to you."

Amber stared at her captor, trying to get a sense of Devin's demeanor. She wondered about her son Jordan if he was alive. "I want to see my son!"

"And you will. I just want your full cooperation and you will get to see him in time," Devin said with a wide smile.

Amber noticed Devin's sincere eyes and his subtle voice that seemed odd. She couldn't believe this man to have a conscience after he kidnapped her.

"What do you say?" Devin asked.

Amber had to play nice. She had no other choice. "Okay,"

"Okay," Devin said with a winning smile. "I will get you your food and if you need anything, you can give me a holler."

Devin got up from the floor and left Amber to her cell. He turned and looked through the top slot opening, like a peeping Tom in heat. To Devin, the feelings he felt were foreign to him. Yet, watching Amber gave him something he never felt before with another person. That was love. He had an idea for Amber to live with him and his family. A perfect life with a white picket fence. He never imagined it would be possible.

Martin stood in the shadows, watching his brother staring at Amber. He knew his brother was infatuated with her. He also knew she had to be eliminated. Martin felt that Devin lost sight of the goal to kill Robert. To avenge their father. But he was determined to do what was necessary to get him back on the path. By removing all obstacles.

"It is time I save you, brother, from yourself," Martin said. "It is the only way. One day you will thank me. Maybe not now, but you will."

Martin heard Sam scream. He went strode by to check on him along with Devin. "Ahhh!"

"Sam it is okay you are home now," Devin said trying to cue his nerves.

"Charles!" Sam yelled.

"Charles is not here," Devin said signaling his brother Martin with a head nod.

"Yeah, he is not here!" Martin said.

"You are lying! I want to see Charles!" Sam demanded. "Charles! Charles! Charles!"

"There are some biscuits, mashed potatoes and gravy on a paper plate by the table. You are welcome to eat it!" Devin said.

Sam gave Devin a cold stare, running toward the food, devouring it with his hands like no tomorrow. "I want to see Charles!"

Sam scarfing down his biscuit, waiting for Devin and Martin's response.

"Get some rest!" Devin said.

As Devin and Martin left the hallway of the confined cells of Amber and Sam, the lights went dark in the instant.

Chapter 18

K enny arrived at Virgil's home. The generic pain pill he took, prior before arriving, didn't do much for his stomach to mask the pain he felt. He had his hand on the right side of the abdomen where Devin stabbed him. Kenny was surprised the stitches held up. He dealt with much worse in both military and law enforcement. Something he and Robert had in common. The most important thing, that mattered more than anything, was to find that serial killer and stop him from committing acts of murder. Most of all, he wanted to protect his son Jamie and his friend Toad.

Virgil Matthews was a twenty-eight-year-old introvert geek that had a strong interest in computers. The closest thing to a girlfriend would be his black laptop he would call Shelly. He was an avid reader that kept to himself and still lived at home, watching over his disabled mother, who had suffered from an accident. That's when he decided to take up an interest in trading stocks on Videx. Virgil made a promise that he would look after her and provide for her. For the past ten years, he did just that.

Virgil's room was surrounded by pictures of domestic animals of male and female lions. Kenny looked to his right only to notice a snake inside a fifteen-gallon tank that appeared to be a brown python coiled in the corner as if it was resting. Virgil's fascination with snake's perturbed him since he never liked them.

After twenty minutes on a laptop, Virgil was able to provide a solid lead, honing in on the Masked Killer's identity based on the license plate information Kenny provided. "What did you get for me, Virgil?"

Virgil chuckled, adjusting his glasses, "Everything uncle John needs."

"Here it is!" Virgil said, pressing the key on his computer, revealing an image of Devin in plain sight. His true face plastered on the screen. Devin Green Stevenson. "6,1' caucasian male. Age thirty-six, black hair, brown eyes. His address is 103 Bolton Drive on Sixth Avenue."

"Did you say, Stevenson?" Kenny asked for confirmation.

"Yes, is there something wrong?" Virgil inquired.

Kenny stood in a rigid stance, taking in the details of Devin's Jawline. His heart thumped as he moved to the side. The sound of knuckles cracked from his fist as if he wanted to punch someone. Virgil was startled by the sound as he turned around from his chair. Kenny's eyes narrowed when he saw an image upon Virgil's monitor. This was the moment for him, the moment of truth that was revealed. His eyes never left the sight of the image from the screen. Kenny walked closer to get a good look at the suspect behind all atrocities of the Redwood murders.

"That didn't take long," Virgil tapped his fingers on his black table. "I'm hearing the Mannequin killer killed over one hundred people. That is some sick shit. What would make someone do all those heinous things?"

"People like that enjoy the act of killing. It gives them a rush, a sense of control over life and death. I should know he tried to kill me twice, with his blade when he stabbed my stomach. I was lucky to survive him if it wasn't for Robert." Kenny sighed.

"Did you tell me about that?" Virgil said.

"Yeah, I was at the hospital for four days," Kenny adjusted his stance, trying to make light of the conversation.

"I don't believe in luck. I believe in miracles," Virgil said with honesty. If this is the sicko behind these killings I'm glad to be of service to help you catch this monster," Virgil turned, glancing briefly at Kenny from his chair. "You still owe me."

"Owe you what?" Kenny asked, turning in his direction.

"You owe me money. Oh, you thought my service would be free? Come now It's time to pony up!" Virgil demanded.

Kenny sighed, sucking his teeth in defeat as he reached for his pants pocket for his dark leather wallet, "How much?"

"Five hundred dollars," Virgil said without falter.

Kenny glared at him, "You gotta be kidding me? Do I look like a bank teller to you? That I can pull that money out of thin air?"

"How much do you have?" Virgil inquired.

"Fifty bucks," Kenny said.

Virgil smirked. "I'm just messing with you. I don't need your money. "But I do need you to catch this bastard and deliver swift justice on his ass. Already six people in my neighborhood have gone missing, including Jordan Maxwell."

"You know Jordan Maxwell?" Kenny asked.

"Yeah, he and I are best friends. The last time I saw him was at a party

"Virgil, what else did you find?" Kenny asked, arms folded.

"Nothing else unusual except this," Virgil pressed on the key on the laptop that revealed information about Devin's job and the profession as an artist.

Kenny's eyes widened to a startling revelation that Devin worked for the Lance Exhibition on the East side of Redwood.

"That explains everything," Kenny said. At least, now I can find this bastard."

"I told you it would be a piece of cake to crack," Virgil gloated. "So, are we good?"

"Yeah, we are good. Can you print that information out for me?" Kenny asked politely.

"Yeah, no problem!" Virgil typed a command key, using the touch screen to guide the arrow and select the option to print from the laptop. The black printer hummed, making clicking noise until it started printing paper from the bottom tray.

Kenny was interrupted by a sudden knock at the door.

"Virgil!" A woman called out to him.

"Yes, mom?" Virgil replied.

"Kandice just called; she wanted you to call her back. She said something about meeting you at the Dinner."

"Oh, shot I totally forgot thanks, mom, for telling me I will call her back," Virgil said.

"Is your friend staying for dinner?" she asked.

"I'm afraid I can't stay. I have to head back home," Kenny said, grabbing the paper from the printer. "Thanks, Virgil!"

"Hey anytime if you need anything else, just let me know," Virgil said, standing up and giving him a pound and a hug.

Kenny went through the door, leaving Virgil's home. He felt his phone vibrate in his pants pocket, walking toward his car on the wet pavement.

"Hello," Kenny said.

"Dad?" Zack said.

"What's the matter? Is everything okay?" Kenny inquired.

"Yeah, I'm okay and everyone else is fine when are you coming back?" Zack asked.

"I'm actually on my way back. I will see you shortly," Kenny said.

"Okay, see you at the house," Zack said. "Goodbye, Dad, love you!"

"Love you son!" Kenny replied.

The moment Kenny got onto the main road, passing stoplights, a dark car was trailing him on the bright moonlight.

* * *

Devin was sitting on a dark beat up comfy couch as he turned on the TV from his hidden room. The walls were surrounded by plastered newspaper clippings on the wall of Robert Maxwell. Some black and white photos. He whistled and gloated on the fact that the police department uncovered forty bodies buried at the park site of downtown Redwood. He noticed a new Lieutenant by the name of Thomas Thorn at the scene, talking to the press gracefully.

Devin glanced at the middle-aged man in his black suit. He was changing the bandaged bullet wound from his right arm he received from the last encounter with Kenny. Devin used a brown bottle that he poured into the cap. He dabbed the liquid against his wound as white foam formed and burned. Devin clipped down his teeth as his eyes closed, breathing lightly. He finished changing the bandage and got up from his comfortable couch. He strode to the door, walking down the wooden steps. His shoes creaked at each tempo. Devin flicked up the light switch and glanced to his right only to find his latest victim on a brown table strapped down with black thick ropes. It was Justin's daughter Casey. A young blonde petite teenager with blue eyes wearing blue jeans with a white t-shirt.

"Please, I don't want to die," Casey pleaded.

"Hello Casey," Devin cooed at her, tugging and rubbing her blonde hair.

"Everything is gonna be alright," Devin said, rubbing her blonde hair.

Casey shivered in fear. Her knees buckled. "I don't want to die."

Devin smiled and kissed her forehead. Casey's cries vibrated from her voice. "I don't want to die!"

"I'm not going to kill you," Devin whispered in her ear, caressing her neck with his rough hands.

"Shhh!" Devin said, putting his finger over her lips. "There, there is a child. I will take care of you. I know you must be starving. You want something to drink? I got a cold bottle of water and a roast beef sandwich with your name on it. Do you want to eat?"

"Yes," Casey said outright.

"Okay, I will get you your roast beef drink of water. There are rules that have to be followed here in this place. If you do, I make sure you are treated with the most care. But, if you disobey me, you will suffer, understand?"

"Yes," Casey replied.

"Rule one you must not call home. Rule two you can not leave this place. If you do, my dogs outside, on command, will devour every square inch of that body of yours. Rule three you will not call the cops. Rule four if you ever try something with me, you will end up like the others." Devin pointed to the right of Mannequins that appeared to be lifelike. He walked over and turned on the light shining at the display.

A cold chill crept up Casey's spine after looking at the victims of Devin's display. Her eyes widened as she gasped at the sight of her father. Well preserved like a mannequin doll. Weight of tears streamed down Casey's face as if a wave of sorrow swallowed her whole.

"Five, if you follow the rules, this won't be your fate." Devin pointed to her father. "Now that you understand the rules, I can go and get you your dinner now."

Casey's cries echoed throughout the room. Her heart shattered to a thousand pieces. Knowing full well her chances of escape were reduced to zero.

"I think we understand each other well," Devin said with a half pretend grin.

Devin left the room with only one thing in mind, getting Jordan ready for the final trial.

Chapter 19

Robert and Katie traveled through the derelict halls. Shattered glass merged with their footsteps. The light beamed above them flickered. They were in partial darkness, passing through the wreckage of fallen mercenaries and broken wooden furniture and tables. Within three feet, bullet holes were more evident in spasmodic patterns from the walls.

The smell of burnt flesh flared up in the air, giving off a charcoal-like smell. Thick blood piled on the floor that smeared at every corner of the wood ruined polish. Katie's nose crinkled up in disgust as she covered her nose. Robert ignored the smell and kept on moving from the halls while keeping an eye on Katie. She struggled in her movement. Her legs felt like weighted cinder blocks after being held captive in that metal and glass death trap. What seemed like hours in that containment, was more than an eternity. An eternity she doesn't want to relive again.

Katie was stiff in her movement. Her heart hardened from the cruel experience she underwent from Devin's hand. Katie turned her head to the right, making sure no one was following them. The idea that her life could end by the blink of an eye, frightened her even more. Her body felt tense from the hot wax burns on her arms and shoulders. All she thought about was how hopeless she was. Unable to escape the truth that she would've been another victim. Katie tried to put up a facade that she was strong and nothing phased her. But Robert sensed something was off from the way she held herself. Somehow he was able to detect a crack in her armor. The half-smiles, the denial was even more apparent.

Katie took a moment to pause. "Did you do all this?"

"I did what I had to do. We got to keep on moving," Robert said.

"Were you able to find Jordan?" Katie said.

Her question stung at Robert like a set of knives, splintering off at his soul. "No, the sick bastard still has him and Amber. But I will find them. They have to be still alive."

"What makes you think that?" Katie asked.

"Because he is playing a sick game and wants me to suffer for my past," Robert said.

"What could you have done to him that set him off?" Kattie inquired looking at his eyes.

"Let's just say I killed his father twenty-five years ago," Robert said. "Do you remember RJ's case?"

"Yes, I read about that case report that you had written many years ago," Kattie said. "Go on."

"Then you know, at the time, I was a rookie cop and my mentor and partner Ronald Decan--" Robert paused, taking a breath. "Got killed by RJ and I went into that warehouse building and fired five rounds into the man when he came at me with a knife. He hit the hard floor without fail. When I stood over RJ's body, with my gun out, there was an emptiness in his eyes. No spark of life. Just silence." Robert's left hand trembled. "There was nothing I could have done to save Ronald. The prick butchered him into pieces. He was barely recognizable. It was bad enough I had to go to Ronald"s house and tell his wife and two children at the doorstep that he was dead while looking them straight in the eye. Yes, I killed the man who killed Ronald, but his death didn't patch up the wounds of his family. Ronald is never coming back to them. My regret was not following behind him when he told me not to." Robert cliched his jaw.

"I'm sorry for your loss," Katie said, reaching for his shoulder for comfort.

"That was a long time ago," Robert said. "I try to honor his memory by catching creeps like this psycho. Sometimes I wonder when will it end? We caught one killer today and another one pops up."

Robert didn't care that Katie took him off the force. In all accounts, he lived with a set code of ethics of not leaving their own behind despite everything. The same principles he was taught in the army still stayed with him to this day."We are almost out here just a little bit longer."

"I don't know if I will make it," Katie said, breathing hard

"Nonsense, we are gonna make it Captain. I didn't come all this way to give up and I'm not going to do that now. We are not that far from the car. Once we get there, we will be out before you know it."

Katie started to lose her equilibrium, but Robert went back in time and caught her by the waist. "Captain, are you alright?"

"Just having some trouble with my legs," she chuckled.

Roberts looked around his surroundings," It is clear so far."

"Don't jinx it now, Robert," Katie said leaning on him.

"Why would I do a thing like that?" Robert asked, teasing her.

"Because I know you," Katie said. "You always seem to have a death wish."

"What is that supposed to mean?" Robert asked.

"Ever since you had been chasing this serial killer, you've been on edge. Bodies piled up."

"I promise, Katie," Robert said with a smirk, winking his eyes. "So, would that mean I get my badge back?"

Katie laughed. Her face flushed with a smile.

"What's so funny?" Robert asked.

"If we get out of this alive, I will reinstate you."

"If that is a fact, I want a pay raise," Robert demanded.

Katie looked at Robert as if he had two heads. Her eyes are burning like the sun.

"It is only fair," Robert said. "And besides I got a debt to pay."

Robert kept his eyes forward. Cool air slapped them in the face from the wall opening. They walked through it in the open darkness. Cold breaths escape their mouths. Katie's body started to shiver because of the cold. Robert took off his black coat and wrapped around her with grace.

"This will keep you warm. Are you alright?" Robert asked, looking into her eyes.

"I've had better days," Katie said.

They kept walking forward, treading the wood panel floors. Robert glanced up the top and noticed a camera above them. He had a feeling Devin was watching them.

"I suppose we are gonna wait for a while when we get a new police station," Robert said.

"What happened to the police station?" Katie inquired.

"Let's just say our Masked killer destroyed the building. Both the FBI and our brothers and sisters of blue met an untimely end," Robert explained. "Among the dead, I saw FBI Director David Swanson, laying face down with a hole in his skull. I was lucky to escape the fire and explosion."

Katie wished she ever asked that question. Her facial expression, from her face, went from happy to sad in mere seconds. Robert met her eyes briefly. Then, he redirected his focus to the path they had to travel. "All these lives lost and I wasn't there to prevent it."

"Don't sell yourself, short Captain. There was no way of knowing how things would turn out. It was good you weren't there." Robert tried to block the whole incident from his mind. The amount of death he witnessed, tugging at his heart. All the screams of the fallen echoed from the back of his mind like a nightmare that never ended. The pain he felt can't be erased, nor can he shut the screams and death that circled him throughout his twenty-five year former career in law enforcement.

A shadowy figure walked behind them, wearing a dark camouflage. He watched Robert and Katie move further toward the room where the car was located. He gripped his custom-made knife with a dark hilt. He moved at a slow pace observing them. His green eyes are lasered. He clenched his teeth, imaging the attack in his mind re-hearsing

Robert glanced at the opening of the wall of the room, he escaped from the crazed mercenary with a flamethrower grenade launcher. In the line of his sight, he noticed the red car. The same red car that held him captive before the trials. "There's the car, come on, let's go and get the hell out here."

The man in camouflage strode forward with his knife ready to stab.

Katie turned around and saw the man coming at them with a knife. "Robert behind you!"

* * *

Katie stood back. A struggle ensued between Robert and the mercenary in the camouflage. The mercenary lunged his knife forward, trying to slash Robert's throat. Robert dodged to the side, avoiding the sharp blade. Robert pointed out his gun. The mercenary kicked Robert's gun out his hands before he got a shot out. The mercenary lounged his knife forward, cutting Robert's right arm. Robert stood back putting distance between and the mercenary. He removed his belt and wrapped around his right hand with the silver belt buckle exposed, using it as a defense against the knife-wielding maniac. Robert kept his eyes on his opponent, swinging his belt. He circled him, waiting for the opportunity to strike.

When the mercenary lunged forward, Robert whacked him several times in the head with the belt buckle. The mercenary backed away blood oozing from his head as he whipped the blood off with his free hand.

"You killed my friends," the mercenary said, glaring at Robert with hatred.

"Well, they tried to kill me," Robert said. "Now, I am going to give you a chance to walk away. You don't have to do this!"

The mercenary laughed. "Yes, I do have to do this. Once I'm done with you. I will take care of your girlfriend."

"Walk away!" Robert commanded. "You don't have to do this."

Katie saw Robert's gun five feet from the floor; she went for it and picked it up.

"Last chance!" Robert said.

The mercenary lunged forward with his knife. "I am not backing down. I'm getting my money!--"

Two shots were fired, two bullets hit the mercenary's back, The mercenary hit the floor like a ton of bricks. Katie's arms tensed, holding the loaded gun, inching off the trigger finger. Her eyes paused as if suspended in a picture frame.

Robert turned him over to the mercenary, barely conscious."Where is the Mannequin killer? Tell me!" Robert leaning down gripped his shirt.

The mercenary smelled with blood in his mouth. "I don't know," his voice, barely audible.

"Robert, let's just get out here," Katie suggested.

"I'm not leaving until he tells me what I want to know!" Robert said.

The mercenary ceased. There was silence as blood continued to spread on the floor. "No, dammit!"

Robert was desperate to find answers. But what he got was a dead end. He worried about Jordan and Amber. The thought of them being dead and laid six feet under sent razor-sharp chills to his heart. He wasn't gonna stop until he found them.

"Let's get off here," Katie said walking toward the car.

Robert laid the mercenary back on the floor. "Yeah, I'm coming, but I'm driving."

Robert got in the driver seat, taking out the compartment between the wheel of the car. He took his time to hotwire the car by taking two wires together to start it up. After five attempts, rubbing wires together, the car started. Robert pressed down on the accelerator to rev it up. Katie buckled her seat belt. Robert took the stick shift and moved the gear from park to drive. He pressed his foot on the gas and plowed through the opening of the wall like a bat out of hell.

A cell phone vibrated in the car. Katie picked it up from the tray.

"Hello," Katie said.

"The game is far from over Captain Cambell. I will be seeing you soon," Devin said. He hung up on her.

"Who was that?" Robert asked.

"It was him!" Kattie said, gasping for air. "He said he will be coming from me."

"No, that is not gonna happen. I'm going to take you to a place that will keep you safe," Robert said. "He will not find you."

Chapter 20

K evin arrived at the safe house. The mysterious car that followed was parked five blocks from him. He clenched down his hand on the steering wheel with his right hand. Kevin got out of the car with his groceries. He walked on the dew cut lawn. From the distance, Martin watched Kevin, going toward the safe house with a bag of groceries. The wind picked up in the air and Kevin turned his head to the side, watching his surroundings. No one was in sight. The sound of crickets echoed throughout the night. He went inside, closing the door. Kevin tapped on the keypad and entered the passcode numbers for the alarm system. The keypad blinked to a solid green.

"Hey, I am back," Kevin said, walking toward the kitchen.

"Welcome back, I hope you don't mind. I helped myself to your fridge," Jennifer said, preparing chicken salad in a bowl.

"No, it's alright," Kevin said while putting the grocery bag on the counter. "Where's Jamie and Toad?"

Jennifer replied. "Oh, Toad is asleep and Jamie is in the other room looking after him. I heard him read a bed story to him."

Kevin went over to check the window, peeking through the white blinds. "Hey, did you see anyone come around here?" Kevin took items out of the bag and placed them in the refrigerator.

"No, I didn't, why?"Jennifer asked, feeling concerned. She stirred the salad with a fork while adding salad dressing.

The mysterious car was still parked in the same location. The engine ran cold. Martin hid in the shadows as if he was on the hunt. He adjusted the rearview mirror, combing his hair. He whistled and reached for his golden mask that reflected his dark clothes.

"I'm just asking. It is probably nothing. I am heading upstairs to check on Jamie and the boys," Kevin said walking away.

"Okay," Jennifer said, opening the fridge for a bottle of cold water. She opened the top and drank from the bottle, swallowing the cool fluid down her throat.

Kenny strode toward the hallway. He walked up to twenty-four steps while grabbing hold of the black rail. As he reached the top, he approached the white door, turning the gold doorknob. The door creaked slightly as he opened it. Kenny saw Jamie with Kevin laying on his stomach on the red sofa chair with a book in his head. He smiled, taking a blanket to cover them up. Kenny closed the door. He heard a noise in the other room. Kevin walked toward the other door in the hallway and opened it to see Toad watching the movies on the comfortable chair. The room itself

"Oh, hey Mr. Rogers," Toad said, turning his head to the side with a half-smile.

"Hi Toad, how are you?"

Toad sighed, rubbing his hair. "I am alright." He lied.

Kenny sat on a chair next to him. He stared at his eyes. "You know you can tell me anything, right?"

"To be honest, I'm scared. I can't sleep because of nightmares. I can't close my eyes because of what happened to Zack. I keep on seeing him..." Toad became silent.

"I get it," Kenny said. "Losing a friend can be hard. I lost friends at your age. Even during my time at service."

"You were in the military?" Toad inquired," What branch?"

"I served in the US Army," Kenny said, doing a salute with a smirk.

Toad laughed. "That's cool. Do you think someone like me could do something like that?"

Kenny beamed with a smile. "You don't want to join."

"Why not, you did it?" Toad asked. "I bet you have tons of metals, am I wrong?"

Kenny placed his hand on his shoulder. "Trust me, you don't want to do it." His eyebrows frowned in disapproval.

"Why not?" Toad asked, awaiting an answer shrugging Kenny's hand. Kenny sighed. "The military is not what it is cracked up to be. I have lost more people than I can count. Yet, here I am. What I'm saying to you is that there are more opportunities to be of service without risking your own life. You don't want to rush your life away. You are young and you got your whole life ahead of you. I don't want you to make the same choices that I did. I was young like you once. I was a high school dropout and got involved in fights. Later on, I worked on getting my GED. When I was eighteen, I made the choice to enlist in the army to get away from a drunk, good for nothing stepfather." Kevin's right hand quivered. He clenched his right fist. "I wanted to be a man, to be independent enough to take care of my mother. One night I came home after the end of service. I found my mother on the floor. She had bruises on her face and was unconscious. I went to her and held on to her. I called 911 and got her to the hospital."

Toad paused for a moment, soaking in all the information that he just heard from Kenny. "Did she?"

Kenny looked at him. "Yeah, she didn't make it. The point I'm trying to make here is that you have a chance to have a better life just like Jamie. I admire the friendship you have with him. In a way, I see you as a second son. You can go to school and become a nurse or doctor. I will support you in any way. Hell, even if you become a lawyer."

"What happened to your stepdad?" Toad asked.

"After the funeral, I never met him again," Kenny explained. "That is beside the point. Just give this some serious thought, okay promise me?" Kenny held his arms up for an embrace.

"I promise," Toad said, leaning in for a hug, closing his eyes.

"Good talk, I will let you watch your movie," Kenny said walking away. He turned around. "Oh, Jennifer made some chicken salad.

You are welcome to come down and get some. I will say this, it smells good." Kenny teased with a smile.

"Thanks," Toad said.

"Don't mention it," Kenny winked.

Kenny walked out of the room and closed the door with a light pull. There was a sudden knock at the door. He moved down the stairs. The knocking continued. Kenny glanced at Jennifer in a surprised expression at her face from the hallway. She started to fidget with her feet and hands.

"You stay right here," Kevin said as he went into the closet to pull out his 12 gauge shotgun from the closet. He reached for his rounds on the top shelf and loaded it into his gun.

The knock at the door happened again. Kenny walked to the door, his weapon forward, his eyes focused. He gave Jennifer the hand signal to hide. He looked through the round small window of the door. He sighed in relief at who he saw. Kenny lowered the weapon and opened the door.

"It's okay Jennifer, it's Robert," Kenny said. "You look like shit! He hugs Robert with one arm. "I am glad you are safe."

"I too am Jennifer around? How is Kevin?"

Robert smiled. Kenny let go of Robert allowing him to walk through the halls.

"Yeah, she is around the corner and Kevin is sleeping. He is safe with Jamie," Kevin replied.

Katie walked inside the safe house, getting a sense of her safe haven.

"Oh, hey Captain," Kenny said, adjusting his stance and tone.

"No, need for that Kenny," Katie said. Kenny closed the door behind me."May I use the bathroom?"

"It is down the hall on your left," Kevin explained.

"Thank you, Kenny," Katie said.

Kenny was staring at her. His eyebrows raised. He never saw Katie fearful before. It worried him. He made the decision to keep an eye on her.

"Jennifer," Robert called her.

"Oh, my god!" Jennifer said, hugging him.

"Where are Jordan and Amber?" Jennifer asked.

"The killer still has them," Robert said.

"You said you will do everything in your power to find them," Jennifer said.

Kevin walked in on their conversation. "I got some news for you Robert, I think you want to hear it."

"Okay, let's hear it," Robert said.

"I got the ID on the Masked Killer," Kenny said with a confident tone.

Martin dialed his cell phone standing behind the bushes near the safe house. "I found the man you told me about. He is with Robert."

"Good brother, come home we have much to plan," Devin said. Martin hung up the phone. His eyes bulged at the sight of Jennifer, watching from the window. His breathing became heavy as carbon dioxide exhaled from his breath as he walked away.

* * *

The Royal Eight bar thrived with many customers. Some want nothing more to exceed their bar tap. The open neon flashed from the outside. Barbara Smoke was working a double shift, serving multiple customers food. She was in the back in the kitchen, washing beer mugs in the sink in cool water with motorized bushes. Barbara used non-fat chemical compounds to clean the mugs. She raised two mugs at once and placed them on the tray to dry out.

"I can't believe Nathan is dead," Barbara said. "Who is going to run this place, Wendell?"

"I was thinking it would be you," Wendell replied. "You have more experience than any of us, which would make you more qualified."

"I don't know?" Barbara said.

"I know you, Barbara, you can run this place, trust me on that," Wendell said with a smile. "Hey, if you don't want to do it, I can easily fill in the spot."

Barbara arched her eyebrows and fiddled with her hair with a small. "Okay, I will give it a shot."

"Hey, I need some pretzels!" One customer yelled in a drunken stupor.

"I got it, boss," Wendell said, walking out to face the crowd.

"Barbara Smokes, owner of the Royal Eight bar. It does have a nice ring to it." She smiled with pride.

After closing the bar, Barbara walked out of the bar to her car. She reached into her black purse for her key fob to unlock her door.

"Hey stranger," Martin said with a mild tone.

Barbara dropped her keys as she gasped. She turned around and realized it was Martin. Martin leaned over and picked up her keys. He passed her the keys.

"You gave me a freaking heart attack," she said.

"Sorry about that, how are you?" Martin asked.

She glanced at him. "I'm okay, Martin. What are you doing here?"

"I am just visiting an old friend," Martin said.

"That's bullshit! You burned down that bridge a long time ago," she scoffed walking to her car.

Martin walked in front of her car. "Barbara, I regret how things ended with us. I want to try to get to know you more. Please, I would like to try. Let me at least make it up to you. Have dinner with me."

Barbara rolled her eyes. "I need to get going. Good night, Martin." She gets in her, starts it up. Martin knocked at Barbara's car.

Barbara pressed the power button to roll down the window.

"Just think about it," Martin said. "Okay, no pressure."

Barbara sighed. "Okay, I will think about it."

Martin smiled," Here, let me give you my number."

Barbara pulled her cell phone out and added Martin's number on her contacts list. "I got it."

"Okay, Good night Barbara," Martin walked away.

"Good night," Barbara replied as she drove off.

Martin never imagined he would encounter Barbara again. She was the closest thing to a friend. Like his twin Devin, he yearned for a connection to another soul. Someone who challenges him in every way. Barbara Smoke was not just a pretty face or the typical damsel in distress; she was an ambitious fighter. When Barbara saw something she wanted, she would get it. These were the qualities he was looking for in a mate. He decided to leave and meet with his brother. Robert Maxwell would be in for a rude awakening from the twin's sordid little schemes that were yet to come.

Chapter 21

The piece of the puzzle revealed. Robert knew this was his one chance. His mind raptured at the thought of Jordan and Amber's suffering. Katie and Kenny paused as their eyes locked. She directed her attention to Robert.

"Are you sure it's him?" Robert asked, looking at Kenny.

"The person behind all those killings is Devin Green Stevenson. The son of RJ Green. My sources don't lie, Robert. I'm sure of it," Kenny said.

"I say we find Devin. Do you have his address?"

"Yes, I do," Kenny said. "I have all that covered."

"Okay, then we need a way to get inside his place. Jordan and Amber have to be there," Robert replied.

"I can make a few phone calls," Katie said, tying her blonde hair into a ponytail.

"No, we go out on our own. We don't need more police being killed in elaborate death traps," Robert said. "We do this off the books. Are you in?"

"Yeah, I'm all the way in," Kenny said. "How about you, Katie?"

Kattie nodded her head. "Yeah, count me in." It would be best if we do a full property search on who owns what."

"Sounds like a good plan," Robert. So, Kenny and I will leave tomorrow morning to meet up with Devin Stevenson," Robert said. "Captain, you can fill us in on the details of the property. Now, we all should get some rest."

Jennifer heard their conversation from the hallway. She leaned back from the wall when Robert approached her. "So, you and Kenny are going out?"

"Yes, that is the plan. I will find Jordan and Amber and I will bring them home," Robert said, looking Jennifer in the eye.

Jennifer paused for a moment.

"Jennifer, is there something you want to say to me?"

"No, just be careful and make sure you bring Jordan and Amber back in one piece," Jennifer said heading up the stairs.

Robert observed Jennifer and he felt there was more she was not telling him. He didn't push the issue. He sighed and collected himself. Robert yawned, stretching out his arm. He checked his watch and it was eleven fifteen.

Kenny tapped Robert on the shoulder. "Looks like this is it, Robert. Are you ready?"

"I was born ready. This was what I meant to do. On that note, I'm off to bed. Have a good night, Kenny."

"You too, Robert. I have a feeling this is our guy."

"I know what you mean," Robert replied.

Robert walked toward his bedroom on the second floor. The air conditioner was circulating through the air. Robert held his hand to his head, feeling the weight of sluggishness throughout his body in each step he took. He entered a room, closing the door behind him. The room had a brown dresser, a mirror on the wall, and a medium-size lamp. Robert plummeted himself on the bed staring into a grey dull wall. It was silent.

The stillness of the night resonated with Robert's inner torment. The hollow empty void of darkness surrounded him into a blanket. He sighed, soaking in the sorrows. The helplessness Robert felt was unending for him, knowing that Jordan and Amber were being held captive in a sick twisted game. Robert knew there were more trials he would have to endure to save Jordan and Amber. He reached for the remote to turn on the TV. The first image Robert saw was a female reporter, stating news headlines of more gruesome bodies that were uncovered behind a derelict library in downtown Redwood Park Ave.

Yellow caution tape was plastered in each corner of the library. It would take time for forensics to determine the identity of the victims without dental records or thorough DNA. Sometimes Robert wonders how many people like Devin walked the street, blending in with the public, how many murders become cold cases go unsolved, and how they get away free and repeat the same offense.

After capturing and busting forty-five offenders, he thought the wheel wouldn't end. More and more killers like Devin would come out of the woodwork. There was no quick-fix solution. He had a job to do and that was to serve and protect. Robert remembered the sworn oath he took early in his police career.

It was morning. Robert got up from the bed. He went inside the bathroom to get himself prepared for the big day. Robert heard the TV come on in his room. A familiar voice was heard from the monitor. "Hello, Detective Maxwell, did you sleep well?"

Robert walked out of the bathroom and saw Devin in his golden Mask, wearing his signature dark hood. "What's wrong Detective Maxwell, the cat caught your tongue? You have a nice place."

Robert reached for the remote to change the channel. It was futile since Devin was on every channel.

"I wouldn't change that channel if I were you," Devin said.

"What do you want?" Robert restored.

"I think you know what I want," Devin said. "Your fifth trial will be soon. Your son Jordan and Amber will make a guest appearance on your last and final test. I'm looking forward to our reunion. See you soon. Devin laughed.

Robert glared at him with hatred. "I'm coming for your ass. You hear me! You're fucking dead!"

The monitor went dark. Robert threw the controller against the wall as it shattered against the wall. Kenny knocked on the door and Robert gasped, pulling out his gun.

"Is everything alright?" Kenny asked. "I heard some noise."

Robert placed his gun back into his black holster. Kenny opened the door.

"Are you alright?" Kenny asked, sensing something was off.

"It was nothing. Just a nightmare," Robert said walking passed him.

"I figured that," Kenny said, noticing the controller on the floor smashed up to tiny bits. He closed the door to Robert's room.

When Robert and Kenny strode to the kitchen. He saw Kevin, Jamie, and Toad on the high raised wooden stool, salmon cakes with buttered grits, and toasted bread. Each of their glasses was filled with Cranberry juice. Smiles were exchanged among the boys. Jennifer was over by the electric stove flipping more salmon cakes on the skillet.

"Good morning everyone!" Robert said. "Where is Katie?"

"Oh, she went out to the store to pick up some items," Jennifer said.

"Okay," Robert said.

"Hi, Mr. Maxwell," Jamie said.

"Hey, Mr. Maxwell," Toad said, waving at him.

"Hey, Papa!" Kevin said with enthusiasm.

"Hey, little man," Robert said, rubbing his head. Robert lowered himself to meet his gaze. "How are you doing today?" Robert smiled at him.

"I'm okay papa when is his dad coming back?" Kevin asked.

There was a brief moment of silence. Jennifer gasped. Her mind drifted to the fact how much she longed for him. How she missed his warm touch. She forced herself not to cry in front of Kevin and everyone.

"He will be back soon, Kevin I promise," Robert said, filling his head with hope.

"You are welcome to eat some salmon cakes, Robert. They are really yummy. Jennifer leaned over to grab her spatula to pick out the salmon cakes; she piled them on plastic deep blue plates.

Jennifer scrambled eggs that had sprinkles of black pepper on. The smell of grits caused Robert's stomach to growl loudly.

"You and Kenny help yourself," Jennifer said. "I'm gonna go get off my feet. You enjoy your breakfast." Jennifer left the kitchen and headed to the living room.

"Let's dig in," Kenny said.

"Yeah, this food looks good," Robert said.

* * *

Hours later. Robert and Kenny arrived at the house where Devin lived. Robert got out of the car. His eyes were zeroing in on the large structural interior design of the white house. A black gate stood before them. Robert walked toward the gate. His mind lost to rage that borrowed deep. He lifted the latch open for Kenny to walk through. They both treaded up the grey rock steps. Robert approached the door. He picked up a silver door knocker and banged loud against the doorknob. Robert stood back and the door opened, leaving a slight opening. A man walked in front of the door.

"Can I help you?" The man asked.

"Yes, we are looking for Devin Stevenson," Kenny said. We are local cops for the Redwood Police Department. "Are you him?"

He came further out into the light. "No, I'm not him. I'm his brother Martin."

Robert gave him a cold serious stare. He never suspected Devin had a brother. He wondered how he wasn't privy to such details. Something didn't feel right about Martin. Robert was keen on that.

"Mind if we come in?" Robert asked.

"Yes, please come in," Martin said.

Robert and Kenny walked with Martin. They both noticed paintings of rare abstract art. There were two marble statues of a man in a robe. One of the paintings captured Kenny's attention that depicted a blacksmith forging a sword.

"That is a nice painting you got there," Kenny said. "This looks like it took place during Medieval times."

"Yes, you are correct. I have a good eye for art I see," Martin said with a smirk. "It is actually one of my favorites. Can I get you, two gentlemen, anything?"

"No, we are okay," Robert said.

Martin went over to sit on the chair. Kenny stood near the wall and Robert sat on the red leather sofa.

"Does Devin own this place?" Robert asked, looking into Martin's eyes.

Martin replied. "No, this house is in my name."

"When was the last time you saw Devin?" Robert asked.

"Four days ago. My twin Devin works at an art school in downtown Redwood, why did something happen?" Martin asked in a concerned tone.

"Do you mean identical twins?" Kenny asked for confirmation.

Martin nodded. "Yes, that is correct."

"What do you do for a living, Mr. Stevenson?" Kenny asked.

Martin smiled. I'm a simple farmer. I grow the best apples in our county. If you want, I can show you around."

"You own another property, Mr. Stevenson?" Robert asked.

"Yes, I do. I own some property. It is in our family name," Martin said.

"Tell me about Devin. How is your relationship with your brother?" Robert asked.

"We are close," Martin answered. "We do everything together."

"Does he have any enemies, friends, or lovers?" Kenny asked.

"Devin didn't have a lot of friends. We have each other. Devin had a girlfriend whose name was Lisa. Lisa Jennings. She was a sight to behold. My brother had good taste."

"What happened to her?" Robert asked.

"I haven't seen her for a while. Lisa and Devin had their moments. But it has been three weeks since I last saw her. That is all I know," Martin said.

"I have reason to believe there is a killer on the loose," Robert said.

"I heard about the gruesome murders from the news. Do you think he was behind the murders? Devin is not what you think."

"Do you know where he works?" Robert asked.

"Yeah, he works in an art exhibit. He looks to make things with his hands," Martin said.

"Tell me more," Robert said.

"His specialty is making sculptures of people and mannequins," Martin said.

Robert knew it was him. The moment Martin mentioned the keyword Mannequin. That made his heart beat faster while masking the intensity of his rage." That will be all for now. Robert gave Martin a white card.

"If you hear from your brother, give me a call when you can," Robert said leaving the house with Kenny.

"Devin is our guy," Robert said.

"Yeah, something eerie about that Martin. What do you want to do?" Kenny asked.

"I say we go and check out this art exhibit," Robert said.

"I will follow your lead," Kenny said. "This time I will drive."

Robert laughed. "Not a chance."

They walked to the car.

Martin called Devin on his cell phone while looking out the window. "Robert Maxwell was here with Kenny Rogers. He asked about you. How do you want to handle them?"

"You don't worry brother, they will be dealt with soon enough," Devin said. "Stick to the plan."

"You got it, Devin," Martin said. "Soon we will have our revenge."

Chapter 22

- -

Above the walls of his cell, Jordan heard footsteps. The sounds started to become louder with each thump. Dust stirred in the air. Yellow wax candles burned bright on a silver candle holder, which was adjacent to Jordan. His nose wrinkled as he sneezed. He feared the worst possible outcome of his situation. Jordan's eyes searched around the perimeter, looking for tools that could be useful in his escape.

As Jordan struggled against his restraints inside a dark cellular shade, he screamed, pleading for someone to help him. Jordan felt like an injured rabbit caught in a booby trap. On top of the wall, water droplets had fallen between the cracks into his head. The droplets of water dripped every two to five seconds. He grew tired pulling against the ropes that held him down. His head rested on the table.

"Please! Anybody out there?" Jordan asked. "Anybody?"

Jordan heard a voice from the other side of the wall. "Hello?"

"Hey, can you hear me?" Jordan asked.

"Yeah, I can," the voice said.

"What is your name? My name is Jordan?" Jordan asked.

"Casey, my name is Casey," she said. She looked through the small window opening of Jordan's cell.

"How long have you been here?"James asked, struggling against his restraints.

Casey cried with a light moan. "I don't know. I just want to get out here, but I can't leave. Not when there are crazy dogs outside waiting to tear us apart."

"Dogs? Do you know how many dogs are out there?" Jordan asked.

"How the hell am I supposed to know," Casey scoffed. "I was told I would have to follow the five stupid rules to live whatever that means?"

"Rules?" Jordan asked, awaiting her answer.

"Yeah, some crazy man told me if I didn't follow them. I would be dead just like my father," Casey said, leaning against the wall crying.

"Casey, I know things are rough. But if we stick together, we can get through this. I'm sure there has to be a way out of this place," Jordan said looking around the corners.

"There is no escape. My father is dead. No one is coming for us!" Casey said in a hysterical tone.

"Casey, do you have a hairpin?"

"What? Why do you need a hairpin?" Casey asked.

"Yes or no? Do you have one?" Jordan inquired.

Casey felt the back of her brown hair. She felt the impression of a hairpin and pulled one out of her hair. "Yes, I got one."

Casey's hairpin was short with a miniature black butterfly attached to it. The hairpin reflected from the light outside the cell.

"Okay, what do you want me to do with it?" Casey asked.

"Good, do you see any locks or any type of key slots?" Jordan asked. "I'm gonna need you to pick the locks for me. I will walk you through."

Casey looked through the opening from the bars for any type of lock. She noticed a latch with a lock on the side, which was five inches from her reach. "I can't reach it. It is too far."

"Okay, I need you to do something for me," Jordan said.

Someone from the shadows reached for Casey's hand. Casey turned around in freight. She stood back. A young boy appeared in front of her, placing his hand over her mouth. He held his finger over his face.

"What's going, Casey?" Jordan asked.

"You have to be quiet," the boy whispered.

"Who are you? Where did you come from?" Casey inquired.

"I am Sam. You have to be quiet. My uncle will come," Sam said.

"Sam, is that you?" Jordan asked.

"Yes, my friend, it is me," Sam said. "I am glad you are okay."

Jordan smiled. "It's good to hear from you."

"I can get us out of here. I made a tunnel that can get us all out of here," Sam said. "We have to move quickly before they come."

"I can't move, Sam. I'm tied up. Do you have anything on that can cut these ropes," Jordan asked.

Sam heard footsteps from when one of his wires were triggered from one of his bells he set up for an alert. "One of uncle's is coming. I will be right back, my friend."

"No, don't go," Jordan said. "Sam, come back!"

Sam moved fast into a small hole on the corner floor under Casey's bed. He placed back up the wooden panel to conceal his exit. He crawled through the tunnel. His elbows and knees moving in synchrony on the dirt. He saw the opening up ahead. A light shimmered in the darkness that gave off an abundance of radiance. Sam placed a flashlight twenty feet in front of the tunnel. He used it as a beacon to guide him through the darkness.

Sam reached the end of the tunnel and clawed his way up out of the floor and into his cell. With effort, he sealed up the hole in a hurry by placing two small wooden panels up in place. Sam brushed the dirt off his clothes and slid under the blankets of his bed. He pretended to be asleep. Sam heard a knock at the door. The door opened letting out a loud squeak. Martin came into his room. He turned on the light and walked to his bed. Martin shook Sam to wake him up.

"Hey, Sam, it's Uncle Martin," he said.

Sam pretended to wipe the crust of his eyes and yawned. He opened his eyes slowly like a slow frame.

"Hey," Sam said.

"I got something for you," Martin said.

Martin handed Sam a paper brown bag. Sam looked at him with curious eyes.

Martin smirked. "Go ahead, open it."

Sam unrevealed the bag and reached inside it. His eyes bulged when he realized it was two sets of toy Mustang cars. One was blue and the other was red. "Oh, thanks, Uncle Martin. I always wanted something like that."

"I'm glad you approve," Martin said.

"When will I see Charles again?" Sam asked.

"I told you this before Charles is not coming back," Martin said.

"I don't believe you!" Sam said, glaring at him.

"I wouldn't lie to you. Believe when I say this, he is not coming back," Martin said. "He would want me to take care of you."

Sam pulled back from Martin's head, "Go away! I don't want to see you again..."

Sam slammed his fists at Martin's chest with both his hands. As he was doing that, Martin held his hands in place.

"You little ungrateful brat," Martin said.

"Where is Charles? Where is he?" Sam asked. "Tell me!"

Martin clenched down on his teeth. His right free hand clamped into a fist. "He is dead."

"What?" Sam said in shock.

"Charles is gone and he is not coming back," Martin said.

"You lie!" Sam said as he started crying.

Martin tried to reach out and comfort him.

"Go away!" Sam said, burying his head into a pillow.

"I'm sorry, Sam, really I am," Martin said. "I promise I will take better care of you."

"You're just as mean as Uncle Devin. I don't want to see you any-more--Just leave me alone!" Sam said, crying aloud.

Martin closed Sam's door. All he heard was the cries of a ten-year-old. Little did Martin know that Sam had stolen his key. This gave him a golden opportunity to free the others from his crazed uncles.

Fifteen minutes later, a door opened in Jordan's cell. Devin with his golden mask walked in with his flashlight shining at Jordan. "What the hell is going on here?"

"Nothing," Jordan said.

"Don't you lie to me, boy!" Devin said, placing a blade against his face.

"I'm telling you, nothing is going on," Jordan said.

Devin made a small cut to Jordan's face. "Bullshit! You better talk now or I will start cutting your fingers. One digit at a time."

"I am telling you nothing is going on," Jordan said, staring at Devin.

Devin took out his syringe with clear fluid from his dark sweater pocket. "I got a better idea."

"What are you gonna do with that?" Jordan asked when he gasped.

"This will put you to sleep. It is time for your next test Jordan," Devin said.

"No, get the hell away!" Jordan pleaded as the syringe went to his arm and Devin pushed in the sedative to put Jordan to sleep.

Jordan's eyes became heavy and drowsy. In more minutes, he was out cold. Casey witnessed what happened. Devin untied the ropes binding his hand's feet that were double knotted. He lifted Devin over his shoulders.

"Hey, where are you taking him?" Casey asked. "Let him go!" She banged on the wall.

"It doesn't concern you," Casey," Devin said. "Remember what I told you. The choice you make can determine your life and death. I suggest you choose carefully, or you will end up in the spot next to your father."

Devin slammed Jordan's door to his cell. He placed Jordan in a wheelchair, strapping his wrist and hands with more rope. He whistled throughout the whole process. "You, Jordan, will be a work of art. I think your father will enjoy your performance in the finale act during the last trial. Your mom and I will be in the front row seats to watch you. So, you won't be alone. When it is all said and done, I will kill your father and take Amber. I was thinking of popping the question to your mother to take my hand in marriage. What do you think? Should I take the risk?"

Jordan still was unconscious as they continued to walk the halls.

"I guess not. Well, I think it is high time to meet your new play dates. You will grow to love them as I did."

Devin opened a door to a room. He flicked on the light from his right. Walking forward, there were several mannequins lined up from right to left of men and women dressed in fashionable clothes.

"My latest work of art. I spent a lot of time shaping and creating all of these wonderful people," Devin said. "I always had a passion for making things. My father never appreciated my gifts or what I was capable of doing. He said it was a waste of time. But little did he know, I would make a name for myself. The Mannequin killer of Redwood. My brother never approved of the title."

Devin stopped for a moment. He picked up a vest from the back of the wheelchair and placed it on his chest. "You will be all set for the main event."

Devin unzipped the side pockets of the vest and placed two small blocks of C4. He then pivoted his foot to reach for the timer that was at the center of the vest. Devin placed the timer on Jordan's lap.

"You are ready for the final trial, Jordan. That is, if your father will be able to survive this challenge. All is in place for the last event. The only thing left is for the key players Kenny and Robert to make their appearance. I love the metaphor of killing two birds with one stone. I'm looking forward to the reunion and it will be a very memorable one," Devin said. "More bodies will hit the floor before this night is over. And they too will be added to my collection."

Chapter 23

Robert and Kenny were at the art exhibit in downtown Redwood, Washington. The engine ran cold when both of them got out of the car, soaking up the air. Kenny puffed his last hit from a cigarette. He threw it on the ground and stomped the life out of it with his shoe.

"I thought you quit smoking?"

"After all the shit that went down, it made me pick up the old habit."

Robert chuckled. "I don't blame you. I haven't smoked in ten years. It was easy to smoke as a stress relief."

"What do you use now to cope?"

"I use a stress ball. It does wonders. If that doesn't work, I try yoga."

"Yoga? I can never picture you doing that."

"It is about balance and condition. Plus, it feels good to get that good stretch in."

Kenny gazed at Robert, "Hmm, I got to try that stress ball if it is that good. At this point, I'm willing to try anything."

"You can also try patches and go cold turkey. I'm just throwing it out there."

"I thought about using it, Robert. I just don't think they would work for me. Maybe the nicotine gums might work."

"That is up to you."

Kenny eyed the front building as they were walking. "I never thought about going to an art gallery of all places. I believe Jamie would love something like this. Hey, umm, I know you and Jennifer are not on good terms. I know it is none of my business, but she's just stressed and worried about Jordan. I heard her cry herself sleep calling out Jordan every night when I was at the safehouse."

Robert collected his thoughts, thinking about his son Jordan. Kenny's words cut deep to his core. Robert couldn't deny the anguish and pain that lingered in his temple as he rubbed his head. The echo of regret stirred at his soul.

"You're right, it is none of your business," Robert said.

"I didn't mean to step on your toes, Rob."

Robert opened the door to the art gallery and Kenny followed behind. They ignored the guest at the table, sipping lattes. Soft music played throughout the halls. On each side, tall walls had exotic oil paintings on display. The red, blue, yellow, and orange of two large paintings caught Robert's attention.

There were dark statues that stood out amongst the people that depicted different animals of wolves and bears. Many men and women huddled together, drinking champagne. All their eyes engaged at the latest work of art.

"Can I help you gentleman?" A stranger probed.

Robert turned and engaged the man with a slight smile."You have a nice painting here."

"Yes, these are two great paintings," Robert said.

"Yes, the two paintings capture the true core of the beginning of creation. Are you familiar with the creation of the universe through Greek mythology? That the universe was born from nothing and into chaos."

"I have to say you have a nice place here, Mr.?" Kenny asked.

"Mr. Frey I am the owner of this gallery. Are you too here to buy any of these paintings? The auction won't start until another hour."

"No, we are two policemen," Robert lied looking at Mr. Frey. His hands clenched. "We are here to find someone. Maybe you can help us, do you know where we could find Devin Stevenson?"

"Oh, Devin. I'm afraid he is off for tonight. He said something about taking care of a family member who is really sick."

"I get it. I understand he is an artist here. I would like to see his work if you don't mind?" Robert asked.

Mr. Frey nodded his head. "Certainly, right this way gentlemen."

Robert and Kenny followed Mr. Frey through the hallway, passing by other people who watched the work of underrated artists. There was one natural-based oil painting that caught Kenny's attention. It was the one painting that had several white birds. These birds glided in the open air as if they were free. His heart raced by the grace of their flight. A part of him felt he was free like the birds. He pulled out his cell phone and took a picture of the painting to show to Jamie. But reality soon hit him clear in the face when he felt a shoulder tap by Robert.

"Try not to get lost," he said.

"Yeah, sure. I'll be alright," Kenny replied.

Kenny placed his cell phone back in his pocket. He adjusted his shirt to hide his gun.

"Right this way gentlemen." Mr. Frey waved Robert and Kenny to come through the door.

When Robert entered the room. He looked around carefully at the glass displays. They were all mannequins. Men and women posing as if on a Broadway catwalk. The creepy part that made Robert's spine cringe was the fact he recognized one mannequin that resembled Nathan Ross. Another mannequin looked like Gabriel Logan, Arran, Jason Diggs, and others he knew that were victims of Devin.

"My, God," Kenny said as his eyes lit up at the sight of horror. Kenny almost barfed at what he saw.

Mr. Frey smiled and glanced at the display in excitement. His lips parted into a half-smile. "Isn't it wonderful? I never imagined seeing something like this." He turned around and noticed how Robert and Kenny reacted. "Are you two alright?"

"No, I'm afraid not," Robert said.

Robert's phone started to ring. He picked it up and saw an unknown caller on the display.

"Hello, Detective Maxwell," Devin said. "I see you are at the art gallery. Did you enjoy my latest work?"

Robert looked around and noticed two cameras. One camera was twenty feet on the wall in front of him and the other camera was located on the right corner, pivoting side to side.

"I can see you and Kenny crystal clear."

"Hello, Devin Stevenson you sick fuck," Robert replied.

"So, you figured out who I am? It doesn't matter. The long game will soon come to an end. I am so anxious to see how your finale trial will play out." Devin laughed. "I'm here with your son Jordan."

"Don't you fucking touch him!" Robert yelled. "If you harm him in any way, I will find your ass and I will kill you."

Devin laughed. "I love it when you are angry. Your blood must be boiling. Rising to the surface. If you want to see Jordan, then you must play my game."

Robert gripped his cell phone lifting his head slightly. He held his hand out in front of Kenny to keep him quiet.

Robert grumbled. "Okay, how do you want to do this?"

"I want you and Kenny to come alone. No cops, no surprises. If you do that, your son will live for now. I will send a text as to where I want you too to meet in two days. Take care, Detective Maxwell." Devin clicked his cell phone off.

"Was it Devin?" Kenny asked, scratching his head.

"Yeah, it was him," Robert said. "Something tells me his game we will be playing won't be easy."

"What makes you think that?"

"Call it a hunch and usually they are not wrong."

Although they were heading for a trap, they had to prepare for the unexpected. Robert had to cling on to hope that Amber and Jordan were still alive. Devin wouldn't kill them right away. Somehow Robert sensed his fifth trial was upon him. Like the hands of a clock, moving with each second he felt his time was near. Whatever sick game Devin was concocting, Robert had to find a way to beat him.

* * *

Barbara arrived at the restaurant called the Pearl. She was well dressed wearing a blue blouse with black pants that matched with her black heels. She walked inside the entrance and was befriended by a waitress.

"Good evening, madam," the waitress said.

"Hi, I am here to meet with a gentleman," Barbara explained.

"Oh, yes you must be Ms. Smoke. Right, this way," the waitress said guiding her inside the dining room.

As Barbara walked further, she saw Martin well dressed in a casual khaki pants blue-collared shirt with a blue coat. He smiled at Barbara when she approached the table and set down. The waitress placed lamented menus in front of them.

"I will give you too some time to decide what you want. Can I get you two anything to drink?" The waitress asked.

"Yes, I would like some water," Barbara said.

"And can I get anything, sir?" The waitress inquired.

"I will have some water too," Martin said looking through his menu.

"Okay, I will be back with your drinks," the waitress said.

"I'm glad you came. You look stunning," Martin said with a warm smile.

"Thanks," Barbara said, flicking her hair back with her hand turning the page of the menu.

"So, how are things with your family? I haven't seen your brother in a while."

"Oh, you know Jacob, always on the constant move from one job to the next. Dad has retired from landscaping and mom she still works as a bank teller. What about your family?"

"Family is okay."

"You don't always talk about family? Why is that?"

"There is nothing much talk about with them. I would like to hear more about your adventures."

"Here are your drinks," the waiter said. "Are you two ready for your order?" The waiter pulled out his pen and notepad from his pocket.

"Thanks, I will let her go first," Martin said.

"What can I get for you?" The Waitress asked.

"I have the Salmon cooked spinach with some coleslaw," Barbara replied. "And I would like to get Cheesecake for dessert," Barbara said.

"Good choice for the Cheesecake. What can I get you, sir?" The waitress asked waiting to jot down his response.

Martin placed down his menu and gazed at the waiter. "I have the roast beef, asparagus, and mashed potatoes with tomatoes. As for dessert, I would like to have the fudge brownies. That would be all."

"Okay, your order will be ready in forty-five minutes," The waiter said, taking their menus and walking toward the doorway of the kitchen.

"You still didn't answer the question about your family."

"My family is fine," Martin explained. "I have been bonding with my brother and my nephew. Tell me something, Barbara have you ever wanted to travel the world and explore?" Martin placed his hand over her hand. "For the first time, I never thought I would have feelings for someone. Until I met you. I don't say this a lot, but I would like to see where this would go."

Barbara smiled, batting her eyes. "I would like to see where this goes too."

Martin smiled back. "I know you will love the food here."

Chapter 24

Devin drove to the Redwood cemetery in his black Mustang. He hadn't been there in two years. The cold air whistled, slapping his face like a ton of bricks. Devin walked up a hill, passing several gray granite tombstones, mausoleums, and other structural buildings that lined up in rows. He and Martin would come by the cemetery to honor their father, the notorious Scavenger killer of Redwood. But this time, it was Devin who came alone to carry out the ritual tribute. A tribute to the man who gave them life and promise. Birds flew overhead. The trees swayed side to side. No one else was around.

The place felt empty, walking across a museum of the departed on the fresh-cut lawn. Even he could relate to the loss which stung deep like an uneven blade that dug into his flesh and can't be removed. After walking for twenty minutes, he stumbled upon the tombstone that was familiar to his sight. He kneeled down with both knees on the grass.

"It's been a long time, father. It won't be long until we get Robert Maxwell. Our revenge will be fulfilled. I promise you." Devin placed flowers on RJ's black marble tombstone.

He took the pocket knife out of his pocket and slit the inner palm of his left hand. Devin's blood dripped all over the bottom of the tombstone as he guided his hand in a circle. "I swear it! Robert will make a good addition to my work."

Devin stood up from the tombstone. A stranger called out to him. "Excuse me, the cemetery is not open. I'm gonna ask you to leave."

Devin was quiet, gripping his pocket knife behind his back.

"Young man, I'm gonna have to ask to leave, or I will call the cops."

"Okay, I'm just here paying my respect to my father."

"I don't give a damn! Trespassers are not invited. It's that simple. Now, are you gonna leave, or I will call the cops?"

Devin turned around to face the man with a smile. He was a tall middle-aged man that had blues eyes with a rough exterior face in rugged clothes."Okay, that is no problem. Maybe you can help me with something."

"Well, leave! I got things to do," the man said. "You can help yourself out of the gate."

Devin walked close to the man with a fake smile sizing him up. In his mind, the old man was nothing but disposable parts that no one will miss, his right hand twitched with excitement.

"Wait! What are you doing? The exit is that--"

He pulled him close for two solid thrusts in the stomach, ripping through fabric and flesh. The man had a shocked expression on his face as he screamed in agony going down on his knees. Before he said a word, Devin placed his hand over his mouth, stabbed his throat, cutting into his jugular vein. He got on top of the man and stabbed the man fifteen times in the chest. Blood splattered all over his clothes. His eyes bulged as the blade kept coming down at an angle. "No, one tells me what to do! No one! You pathetic old man! You had to open your fucking mouth."

Devin got up and kicked the dead man in the head twice, breathing hard, letting out his rage. He whistled, dragging the body on the grass. He checked his pockets, pulling out his cell phone and wallet. He placed it in his pocket.

Devin heard a dog barking outside the cemetery. "My day was perfect until you showed up."

He dragged the body across the gate in the grass leaving a trail of blood. Devin opened the trunk of his car with his key fob. He struggled, lifting the body into the trunk and covered it in a dark tarp as he closed the trunk.

The dog kept on barking by the fence. It moved in circles, growling. More sweat saturated the back of his blue shirt. Devin looked up at the sky as if he was cursed as he got in his car.

The cell phone rang in his pocket. Devin picked up the phone and answered it. "Hello."

"Where the hell are you?"

"I'm paying respects to our father. Today was his anniversary or have you forgotten?"

"Shit! I got carried away. Listen, I will be right there."

"No, need Martin. I'm in the middle of something. I just need you to look after our captives until I return."

Martin thought about Devin's statement. "What do you mean you are in the middle of something? Did you kill someone?"

"What do you think?"

"That is inconvenient, did anyone see you?"

Devin turned around looking from side to side. "No, nobody saw me. I don't plan on getting caught. You look after Sam and the others. I will be home soon."

"Okay, I will."

"Goodbye, Martin."

"Goodbye, brother."

Devin ended his call and placed his cell phone in his pocket. The shimmering heat intensified. He whistled to pass the time while ignoring the barking dog. He took off from the cemetery. The gravel meshed against the tires as he revved the engine, burning rubber. "I know just the place to take care of you, old man. You will be nice and cozy with the others." Devin laughed, turning on the radio on full blast.

* * *

Robert was just alerted of the whereabouts of Devin's chosen place in less than twenty-four hours through a text. He replied to Kenny's cell phone as it binged. They both know good and well it would be a trap. The road ahead wouldn't be paid with good intentions. A sudden inexplicable trigger set Robert off. He tried to shake off his PTSD. The screams, the blood, still echoed at the corner of his mind. Robert was torn between the past and present. What kept him somewhat sane, was the drive to save Jordan and Amber.

"Hey, Rob, you okay?"

Robert held his hand to his head. "Yeah, I am okay. Nothing I can't shake off with a bottle of rum."

"Are you ready for this?" Kenny asked.

Robert's cheek formed into a smirk. "I was born ready. It is time to end this. This time we are gonna take Devin down. It's time we put an end to this."

Katie came into the room. "Kenny, can I talk to you for a moment?"

Robert looked at Katie and Kenny. He knew something was going on between the two but didn't bother to ask. "I will let you two talk. I'm gonna go and get our supplies."

"Okay, partner," Kenny said.

Katie walked by the seat and sat down and she motioned Kenny to sit next to her. He scooted next to her on the chair. The passion in their eyes was evident from the night of the guest house they shared. There was a slight pause between them. An undeniable connection that burned deeper than the depths of the flames. There was no mistake that Kenny took interest in Katie, his hand warmed her face. She sighed in excitement, inching closure for another intense kiss. He paused.

"Hey, about last night. I hope you don't think I'm gonna just hit and run. Because that is not my style. I really like to see where this goes. I mean, if you want to."

Katie blushed with a smile. "Don't get serious on me. Last night was fun and I enjoyed every minute of our downtime."

"What is it then?"

"Just be careful out there. I can't afford to lose you."

Kenny pulled up Katie's chin with his fingers looking into her eyes. "Hey, you are not going to lose." He pulled her in for a kiss.

Their foreheads rested on each other. Kenny held her face, looking at her eyes. "The best is yet to come."

"Smartass," she said.

"When this is done, we go to the guest again and go for another round."

Kattie giggled. "You are too much."

"Don't you know it," Kenny said.

"Just make sure you do something for me," Katie said.

"What's that?" Kenny asked, looking at Kattie.

"Make sure you return to me in one piece," Katie said.

Kenny winked. "Oh, I will be back with a vengeance."

Kattie laughed for a moment which gave her comfort she hadn't experienced in a while since she was held captive all that time in that wax chamber death created for Devin's dark desire. Kattie watched him leave the room not convinced that he would return to him. Kenny met with Robert by the garage.

"You said what you needed to say, Casanova?" Robert said, teasing Kenny.

"What do you mean?" Kenny asked, pretending like he didn't know anything.

"Come on, I know you've been banging the Captain. And I wasn't born yesterday. There is no shame in your game. Hey, I'm not judging."

"Okay, okay you got me. We had sex last night."

Robert tapped Kenny's shoulder. "I knew it. You dirty dog."

Kenny received a text from Jamie that said, "Love you, Dad, come home safe after you kick that killer's ass." A smirk spread across his face.

He replied to the text and said, "I will Jamie, love you too! You look after everyone at the house when we are gone now."

Robert picked a black duffle bag full of weapons and set them inside the open trunk of the car. He took a moment to reflect knowing full well this would be the last chance to see Jennifer, Kevin, and the others. If there was a chance to save Jordan and Amber, he would take it even if it cost him his life. Nothing mattered more to put this nightmare to end the horrors so others would be safe. Robert lost so much from his past and he planned on not letting others die.

"Are you ready to raise some hell partner?" Kenny asked, closing the door to the car.

"I am ready. Kenny, if things go sideways, you make sure Jordan and Amber make it out. Promise me that."

Kenny worried about Robert as he looked him in the eyes. The idea that Robert may die never crossed his mind because he would always come back from horrible events. Somehow he sensed something was different from what they will face together. Whatever awaited their fate, Robert and Kenny must face it together.

"Robert, I know you always come back. You have more lives than a cat."

Robert gave him a serious stare. "Promise me you will make sure Jordan and Amber get out safe can you do that for me."

"You have my promise, Robert I will make sure Jordan and Amber will get out if the shit hits the fan."

Robert nodded. "Thank you. Let's get out of here. We don't want to be late. Something tells me we will be in for a long night."

Chapter 25

‑‑

The luscious glow of light shined from the moon. As the wind stirred in the air, Robert crept inside an old barn not knowing what Devin had planned. He made final prayers, bowing his head as if it was his last night on earth. He closed his eyes for a moment, hoping to find Ben and Amber alive and unharmed. Kenny glanced at Robert with a worried look, but his mind was focused on watching out for surprises. The intensity was building up for Robert. The thought of losing Jordan and Amber frightened him even more. If he lost them, his world would end. Life would have no meaning.

Robert was at the crossroads of no return. But he knew what he was about to do would determine whether or not he would survive the last trial. Kenny stood on the ground with a dejected expression on his face. Katie crept in his mind, his heart thumped for a millisecond. He was torn from the possibility of not seeing her again. The raw passion that burned like amber can't be distinguished from the core. It still resonated at the surface, still stinging at the top of his tongue that was hard to deny.

"Okay, here we go, " Robert said. "Cover me."

Kenny pulled out his guns. "Okay, on three."

One.

Two.

Three.

Robert nodded Kenny to follow him with his armed Beretta's, while he carried a shotgun going inside. Robert's eyes drifted when he came across a horse stable with six horses that surrounded the area that left an unsettling feeling in the air. There were two lanterns that hung against the wall in a single file. A small flicker of light was still lit in each of them. The horses were startled by their presence.

The smell of horse manure made Kenny's face winced as he walked further into the barn. Flies buzzed in the air. Kenny waved them away. Robert walked at a steady pace to calm them down when he lowered his shotgun on the floor and held his hand's up. Kenny watched in awe of Robert's grace like a musical composure at a circus.

"It is okay. No need to be scared, "Robert said trying to calm the brown horse, reaching his hand out to the horse's head.

The horse lifted his head with its dark eyes on Robert. "It's okay."

The horse calmed down, lowering its head to Robert. He patted the horse's head. "It is okay, there is nothing to worry about."

The other horses started to relax.

"Since when you are a horse whisper?" Kenny asked.

Robert smiled turning to the side. He noticed two blue boxes wrapped in a blue wrapping paper by the floor in the corner. One box with a white card stood out with red letters that spelled his name. He picked the box with the card that read open it.

Kenny held his hand on his shoulder as if a warning. "Are you sure it is not a bomb?"

"He wouldn't blow us up. He is looking for the long game, " Robert said opening up the box.

"Oh, man is that--"

Kenny was interrupted by the sight of a severed head that caused him to gasp in disgust. Then, he regained his composure, shaking off the uneasiness. Something about the head gave Kenny the chills. Robert revealed from the box. It was the head of the man Devin killed at the cemetery. The only thing that stood out was the gap of his eye sockets and some of his front teeth were missing and the deeply carved letter a was on his forehead, which signified Devin's handy work.

"It looks like someone got ahead of himself," Kenny said.

"I don't believe that is the only thing he would leave for me. Our killer always loves to leave bread crumbs for me."

"Why not send a postcard then?"

"No, that would be too easy. He enjoys his work."

"A true attention seeker huh, Rob?"

"People like him can't help themselves but seek an audience. He is sending me a message."

"What is he saying then?"

"I'm about to find out."

Robert continued to examine the box and discovered a small black envelope warped in plastic. As he removed the content, he found a black and white photograph of Jordan in some dingy room. His face contorted as if he was screaming. That was not the only thing that caught his attention. He saw what appeared to be C-4 explosives attached to a black vest. His stomach churned by the horrors of his son's torment. The chill in the air evoked rage that burned in his heart. Robert turned over the photo that said, "Open the other box."

"Don't do it, it could be a bomb," Kevin said.

"I have to know what is inside," Robert said. "If Devin wanted to bomb me up, he would have done so already like the police and FBI he killed back at the station."

Robert went over to the box and ripped off the blue wrappings and tore open the top of the box. Inside he saw a cell phone with a yellow note sticker attached to the front screen that read play me. From the screen, he saw Amber up in the corner of some room with her knees crunched close to her stomach. Her hands and arms wrapped around her legs. Amber was looking up and tears streamed down her cheeks. She screamed, pleading for someone to help her. The image went static and switched to Devin in the mask.

"Good evening, Detective Maxwell. I'm so glad you made it!"

"We are here. Now let them go!" Robert said. "Let them go and take me instead."

"No, I don't want to spoil the festivities. And now that you are both here we can begin with our fifth and finale trial. Beyond this room, there is a red door. Go to it."

"And if we refuse?" Kenny asked.

"They die. It's that simple," Devin said. "I'll be waiting."

The phone turned off.

"Looks like we have no choice, Kenny. We have to go through that door. Remember that promise if anything goes wrong you get them out of here."

"You can count on me. I got your back, Robert. Let's get this asshole."

Robert laughed. "You took the words out of my mouth. Here we go."

Robert couldn't let them die. He knew Devin was serious with all cards on the deck. The only thing he wouldn't risk doing which was to not tempt fate with their lives. If there was a way to save them, this was it. For now, he had to play the game and see it through to the end. There was no way out this time and no turning back. The red door was all that stood from their path. Without fail, they walked onward to face unknown horrors that awaited them.

Passing through the door, there was a narrow space as they walked down the steps. Red lights glowed above them from the darkness. Robert approached a steel door. As he twisted the knob, it squeaked, letting out a squealing sound as he had his gun face forward. Inside a large garage. It was filled with battered cars surrounded by broken beer bottles and other forgotten junk no one would think twice of.

Robert walked slowly surveying the area. His hands tensed with his gun when he moved to the side. Something moved in the shadows from his range of sight for a split second. He turned his gun to the right and to the left. Robert headed to the direction where he thought he saw the person in the shadows. The gun discharged as Kenny felt a blade stabbed into his shoulder from behind as he dropped his guns.

The intruder in dark clothing pushed Kenny against the car. He kept on kicking him. Robert clicked his gun to the assault's head.

"Don't you move or I will blow your fucking head to kingdom come. You alright, Kenny?"

"Oh, I had better nights but thanks for asking." Kenny reached and pulled out the knife embedded into his shoulder blade as he groaned pain. He eyed the man who caused him so much pain. The man looked back at him with emptiness in his eyes that was void of life.

Robert removed the hood of the attacker. Looking at him, Robert could tell he was a middle-aged man in his late forties. Judging from his size, he looked like a muscle-bound bouncer at a local nightclub.

"Judgement day is upon you." He turned around with his hands up, starting at Robert. "The sins of the father shall be visited upon the son!"

The man laughed. Robert turned his head and pistol-whipped him with his gun. "Now, you are going to tell me where to find them, or the next thing you will receive will be a bullet to the head. It's your choice." He fired his gun at the man's right knee as he went down on the floor. The sheer sting of the bullet pulsed through his leg. The man looked up at Robert in contempt.

"Now talk, "Robert said.

Chapter 26

R obert helped Kenny to his feet. "Are you alright?"

Kenny grimaced. "I will be okay. I just need a moment."

Robert glanced at the sight where the man stabbed him at that left a deep wound. He wanted to convince Kenny to stay put. Knowing him that wouldn't be an option and the fact he wouldn't leave him alone to deal with psychopaths.

Kenny grunted. "Where is that bastard?"

Kenny went over to the man and yanked back his foot in position and thrust it forward to his stomach. Robert pulled Kenny back before he had the chance to kick him again. The man moaned while sucking his lips.

"Hey, we need him alive," Robert said.

"I am just following rules, " the man said. "I was promised paradise by delivering you two to him."

"You mean deliver us to Devin? Where can I find him? I want answers now!" Robert demanded.

The man smiled with white teeth.

Robert swayed his gun. "Get up! Now, you will take us where we need to go."

Kenny barged into Robert's side, punching the man in the face wanting to bash his skull in with his hands but instead clamped down on the man's throat, cutting off his oxygen. The man's eyes moved up as if trying to breathe. He tried to pull off Kenny's hands, but his grip was too great. The more he resisted, the more Kenny wanted to squeeze harder. "That's for my shoulder you prick! I should break your fucking neck!" Kenny grimaced looking at the man as his teeth clenched.

The man's voice was groggy as he said, "The end is near!"

"I will be happy to end your ass, " Kenny said. "Just say win!" Kenny's death grip intensified.

Robert stepped in arms extended and pushed Kenny back. He pulled Kenny to a small corner. "Kenny, we need him alive."

Kenny glanced at the man and back at Robert. Robert knew from his eyes he wanted to murder the man. He had to keep Kenny's head on straight by reminding him of what was important. "Hey, we can't afford to lose him. He is our way of finding Amber and Jordan."

"We can't trust him. We have to find another way."

"Kenny, there is no other way. We can't waste any time. I don't know about you, but I'm gonna find my son and Amber. I need you with me."

"Okay, if he gets out of line, he is done."

"Alright then, it is settled."

Robert and Kenny strode over to the man but when they approached the area, he was gone. Robert's eyes squinted as he walked
forward with his gun leveled with his shoulders. He signaled Kenny
to circle behind the car. Kenny crept to the rear of the vehicle pointing his gun. He sighed in frustration. "Damn it! He is gone."

"He can't be far. Wait I see something. I think there is a door."

They trudged down through the opening, trampling on the grey
concrete steps. Small yellow kindles were lit on the corner of each
embedded wall. As they reached the bottom step, there was nothing
about darkness. Robert pressed his hand on the light switch. To his
dismay, naked bodies were displayed on four tables, covered in yellow
wax. On top of their heads, letter a's were deeply carved. Eyeballs
were missing from the sockets. Robert's eyes trailed off at the sight
of the bodies of two women and two men. Each of their stomachs
was painted with red numbers from five to eight. A small blue group
of gift-wrapped boxes laid on the edge of the table by their feet.

"What the fuck?" Kenny replied.

"This is worse than a shop of horrors. Be careful not to touch too
many things. There might be a trap somewhere in place." Robert
observed his surroundings; he was intrigued with the box with the
note on it. A part of him felt that Devin was sending him a calling
card.

Robert turned toward Kenny. "Wait right here, Kenny."

Robert walked close to the nearest table with his gun swaying side
by side,seeing his path was cleared. He picked up a dark note written
in gold letters that said "Vae Victis.

Kenny peeked at the note over Robert's shoulder, trying to inter-
pret the meaning. Robert turned in shock, sighing that almost gave
him a heart attack. He passed him the note.

"Don't be sneaking up on me like that."

"What does that mean?"

"Vae Victis was pronounced"wi-wik-tes" it is a latin phrase that
means woe to the vanquished. He is telling us that we are the con-
quered."

"Just fucking great. And what is this saying?"

A monitor came on from the TV screen mounted on the wall,
showing Devin in his iconic gold Mask. "Hello, gentlemen welcome
to my workshop. I hope you enjoy my work."

"You call this work? I hate to see your other projects," Kenny said.

"Enough with the games--- I want Jordan and Amber. I want to see
them now," Robert said, clamping his left hand into a fist. He glared
at him in heated rage.

Devin changed the channel of the TV, showing two side images.
Jordan was in a corner of a room attached with the same C-4 explosives bound by a pole sitting in a chair. Amber was held in some basement huddled in a corner surrounded by four German Shepherds,
barking and growling at her with their sharp teeth. Her face plastered
with terror and hysteria that ate at Robert's heart witnessing the
situation unfold like a domino effect.

"Now, let us begin, Detective. On the table, next to the third body,
you find another letter with a white envelope. It will lead you to your
next journey. See you soon."

The monitor went dark. Robert ripped through the envelope and discovered an address. He crumbled it with his right fist. "Come on, Kenny I know where we are going."

"Where to?"

"To an old asylum."

* * *

Within two hours, Robert pulled up at the Redwood Asylum. Now updated into a mental institution that was renowned for treating the once criminally insane from the eighties.He parked the car taking out his gun adding a clip to it. Robert looked to his side and saw bright lights on what appeared to be coming from the derelict building.

Walking through the shadows of the night, our seasoned ex officers were about to enter the building. Robert had his handle on the door while Kenny was in position. "They have to be in there. Get ready we are going in." Robert kicked the door forward, pointing his gun in the dim light from the checkered floor hallway. Kenny walked slow behind him. He lifted his foot over the trash.

They followed a trail of blood from the white waxed floors, entering the building. Lights flickered on and off. The air was stale that reeked of death. Windows smudged with bloody hand prints. A message "Welcome" written on a wall from the corner of Robert's eye. As they turned right in the hallway, a large steel door stood before them. At the corner of a room, Kenny heard someone scream.

"Wait! Kenny it could be a trap. We must stick together."

Kenny ignored Robert and followed the shrill sound of the halls. He opened the door that squeaked. In front of him was a young girl strapped to a wheelchair with robe and grey tape, covering mouth. C-4 was hoisted around her abdomen. One of her fingernails was removed. She pulled her head back when Kenny removed the duck tape.

"Everything is gonna be alright. I'm getting you out of here."

"I can't be moved from the chair!" she said.

A TV monitor activated in the room. Devin appeared once on the projection. "Hello Kenny, I see you looking well from our last encounter. The young girl strapped to chair is Casey. She will be my guinea pig for this experiment. All you have to do is solve my little riddle and she lives. If you get the answer wrong, the bomb will detonate killing you both. Here is your riddle. What is always in front of you and can't be seen? You have five minutes to solve this riddle." The transmission ended.

"I don't want to die!" Casy said. "Please, please I don't want to die."

The timer on the wall formed, counting the minutes as if a death sentence. Casey's eyes spotted to a man who entered the room. That being Robert. She thought that he was a serial killer.

"What the hell!"Robert said.

"We don't have much time. Can you solve the riddle?" Kenny asked.

"What is the riddle?" Robert asked.

"That whack job said something along the lines of what is always in front of you and can't be seen? Do you know the answer?"

Three minutes had passed. He thought of the question when the timer kept on ticking. A light bulb came on. Robert knew the answer to the question. The future. The answer is the future."

The timer had stopped and the TV screen flashed on. Devin applauded them. "Bravo Detective Maxwell, Bravo! You did well. Now it is time for the main event."

Chapter 27

"All good things must end. Isn't that right, Detective Maxwell? You survived all my trials and the riddles. Not many have the luxury of piecing together the clues. Revenge is so bittersweet. I waited a long time for this moment. Killing your cop friends was the tip of the iceberg. How I would take my time and get my tools to remove their eyes, watching them suffer was a rush. I didn't want that feeling to go away. Taking Amber and Jordan from you was an added bonus. I have to say her hair smells delicious with that light Jasmine fragrance scent. And her skin smooth like cream. I would love to explore her in every way possible. That's if my dogs don't rip her apart like chuck steak. That would be a pity Jordan, on the other hand, I would keep him alive for at least a week and add him with the others. He would make a fine addition to my work."

A sense of foreboding high jacked Robert's mind on Amber. The idea of his son being tortured and covered in wax for some sick joyride turned knots in his stomach as his heart beated faster, clamping down on the gun. Wanting nothing more to find Devin and end the madness.

"What did you do to my son!"

They all had to suffer for your sins. And all of them made a nice masterpiece to my work."

Robert commented, "I was the one who shot your father not them. This is between you and me. Let Jordan and Amber go. If you don't, you will wish you were dead."

Devin chuckled. "But it is time to end the game. This place will be your tomb."

The TV screen became static. The silence in the room kept them on edge. The fact that Devin wanted to pull the curtains on Robert and everyone else, the fact that this would be last night alive. Survival was all that mattered. Nothing was going to deter the mission.

"Get me out of here." She demanded.

Robert pulled his knife to cut the rope. "Don't worry, you will be safe with us."

Casey nodded, trying to control her sobs. She stood up, removing the bomb off her body. Grateful for the rescue she hugged Robert. But drew back because she knew from instinct that their lives were in danger. Someone moved from the shadows side to side. Kenny turned, heading in the direction of where he thought he saw movement. Out of nowhere, a man swung his knife. He spun around dodging the blades entry and fired five rounds in the torso, putting him down. As the life from his eyes drained from his body, blood spread on the floor. Kenny shuffled forward, kicking the man's leg to make sure the person was dead.

"That's the prick who came at me with a knife. Looks like judgement day for you," Kenny replied. "Rot in hell."

Crossing through the corridors, Robert led them out of the room. He checked to see if it was safe to trespass the empty cold halls. "Where are not out the wood's stay close."

As the door creaked, the stale air penetrated his face. The stench of death engulfed the air when Robert saw two dead bodies of patients. Maggots crawled out of their eye sockets, falling on the floor. Their lifeless corpse's lay on both opposite ends of the white floor preserved in yellow cellophane wrap. Letter a's carved deep in the foreheads Robert covered his mouth. The red lights flickered on and off. Kenny and Casey gasped at the site of the departed. She pulled back in fright, bumping against Kenny. Out of nowhere, a man with a golden mask charged at Robert from the side, pushing him to another room. They both struggled for control of the gun. Casey fidget in fright. Her hands cupping her ears. Kenny reached for her shoulders and said, "Wait here."

Kenny ran in Robert's direction, pulling the chamber back in his gun. He heard the screams and gunfire. When he entered the room, Robert leaned over and removed the attackers mask. Not realizing it wasn't Devin.

"Did you get him?" Kenny inquired.

Robert reached for his wallet. "No, it is not him. It is his brother."

"Shit!" Kenny said. "I thought we nailed the fucker."

"No, I think we hit the hornet nest. Get ready for anything. He's got to be close by."

Casey entered the room terrified. Hands over her mouth thinking the nightmare was over. "Is it him?"

"No, it is not him," Robert said.

Above the corner of the wall, a camera monitor watched them. Devin was sitting from the control room, watching the whole event unfold. He pounded his fist at the keyboard, cursing under his breath. His eyes blazed with rage. Knowing his brother was taken from him. "It's not over yet, Detective Maxwell! Tonight you die!" Devin pressed several green buttons on his control board, sealing all the doors to each room.

"What was that?" Robert asked.

"I don't know." Kenny went over to the door and tried to open it. "Shit, the door is locked."

"Wait do you hear that?"

Whistling was heard in the hallway. A blade scratched against the wall. His black gloved hand guided the knife as if it was a paint brush, leaving its mark. He moved into the hallway three rooms from their location. Gripping the hilt, breathing hard. Devin walked toward their direction. The lights started to flicker. He turned the golden knob of the door that was left unlocked.

Out of nowhere, an air vent from the wall came unhinged from the corner. Robert had his gun ready. He pulled his gun back realizing it was a young boy that crawled out. "Who are you?" The boy asked.

"Robert."

"It's not safe my uncle is mad. He is coming. Follow me, I can get you away from him."

"What is your name?" Robert asked.

"My name is Sam. You have to hurry, he is coming!" he said. "He hurts people bad."

"I think I hear him coming. Casey, you go with Sam," Kenny said.

"No way, I can't leave you," she said.

Sam went back into the vent from the wall, he waved them to follow him.

"I think I hear him coming. Casey, you go with Sam," Kenny said. "Robert and I got a score to settle with this creep. Go on now."

Casey went into the vent with Sam. Kenny closed it up. He pulled his gun out from his holster and hid behind a wooden shelf with Robert.

Devin reached for his machete with a silver tip above the mantle. He held the blade in position moving forward through the door. His arm was ready to swing. As he entered the room surveying the quarters. Devin glanced around the corners. Robert pushed the shelf down when Devin jumped out the way, dropping his blade. Kenny pointed a gun to the back of his head, while reaching for the machete.

"Don't you fucking movie," Kenny said. "Drop the knife and kick it to the side. Do it!'

Devin got rid of his knife.

"Hands up!" Kenny said. Stand up slowly."

"Where are they?" Robert asked, removing his mask.

Devin's cold eyes stared deep into Robert. "You are wondering about your son Jordan, detective?" he smiled. "I can see it in your eyes, the desperation. The guilt that eats you up inside. The fact that your son is held captive for my....work."

Robert pulled back his fist and punched him in the face, took him by the neck, and slammed his head against the wall. He turned him around and punched him hard in the face again and again kneed him in the stomach. "Tell where they are?" Robert had his hands locked into his throat.

"Tell me!"

"You failed them, Detective Maxwell. When you were boozing around, bedding many women, bringing them to Amber's bedroom. And to think she had to sleep in these same sheets. I spent a great deal of my time watching you and Jordan. How broken it was for him to come home one day and to witness you in the arms of young women in Amber's bed. Riding you, soaking up sweat. Yet, you were not aware that your son came home earlier from college. You are no hero. You are just like me. A killer! I never forgot the look on your face when you killed the mercenaries. You didn't even blink."

Devin took out a small switchblade knife hidden underneath the black sleeve of his sweater. He threw the blade at Kenny's right arm with accuracy, disabling his arm holding the gun as it fell on the floor. He tackled Robert on the floor and reached for his gun. They both struggled over the weapon. Devin slammed his hand, trying to get him to drop the gun. Kenny took the blade out, clutching his teeth in agony. He tried reaching for the gun on the floor to get a clear shot but couldn't since his partner was in the way, rolling back and forth. Devin rolled on top, punching Robert in the face.

"You will never find them," Devin said, decking him in the face again and stabbing him in the stomach with his spare blade as Robert screamed. Devin took off running.

Kenny fired three shots at Devin but missed due to his zig-zag maneuver. "Fuck!"

Robert yanked the blade out of his stomach, closing his eyes, trying to block out the pain. Blood was seeping through his white shirt. He stood up slow. He walked over to Kenny, leaning against the wall. Robert reached out his hand to take his gun.

"Go get that son of bitch," Kenny said.

Robert nodded and went on to pursue Devin going through the hallway. He moved through the white floors. The lights were dim.

"Give it up, Devin there is no way out!" Robert said.

"I'm just getting started!" Devin said, running from the side, swinging his axe at Robert's head as he missed him hitting the wall. He kicked the gun out Robert's hand. He drew at his knife in a stance. "It's time to finish this!"

Robert formed both of his fist, ready for combat. His eyes sharp keen on his movement. When Devin lunged forward with the knife, he countered with a quick hold of his forearm. Then, twisted his wrist and arm. Robert punched him hard in the face with two lightning fast jabs to the face. Devin stumbled backwards.

Robert flinched in pain because of his wound. "Tell me where they are!"

Devin licking the blood from his lips," That's the million dollar question, Detective Maxwell. Do you remember the video I showed you with your family? That was taken last week?"

"Last week? What are you saying? Where are they dammit!"

Devin laughed. "They are closer than you think. I will show you."

Robert's heart tugged at him. Coming through fruition of reuniting with his family gave him a small glimmer of hope. Each breath he took felt like daggers piecing his core. But he wasn't willing to trust Devin on his words. Far as he knew, it could be another elaborate trap. Devin opened a brown door with a silver knob as they entered the room. As Devin flicked on the light switch on the wall, Jordan and Amber crooked their heads up to Robert with black duct tape covering their mouths. Both of them facing opposite of one another, sitting on wooden chairs with their wrist and feet bound by black rope.

Devin took steps over to the shelf and pulled out a gun. "Now is time for your final test. Which one should I kill since you killed my brother and father. It is only fair." Devin pointed his gun back and forth evoking moans and trepidation between Jordan and Amber.

"The life for your son or Amber."

"No, you take me. Let them go!"

Devin aimed the gun toward Jordan's head. "That is not how we play the game. You must choose quickly or I will choose for you."

Robert's body froze in fear, having to sacrifice one life for the other. Devin nodded his head. When he was about to pull the trigger, Robert jumped him, pushing the gun up, punching Devin cold in the face. Devin grabbed hold of Robert's wound and hit him with the gun in the head as he fell on the ground. Devin grunted directing the gun to him.

"Just for that-- I'm gonna kill your son first!" Devin said. "Revenge is mine!"

After a few minutes, Kenny entered the room and rolled his gun to Robert on the floor. With quick relaxes, Robert turned and fired three shots at Devin from the chest, arm, and leg as he fell back with his gun motionless. A hard sigh escaped his dying breath. Then, everything went black.

Chapter 28

The nightmare was over and the weight placed on Robert had been lifted. He removed Jordan and Amber's restraints. Jordan got up from the chair and hugged his father which seemed like forever. Amber stood up and held her hands in the embrace, joining in with a hug. Kenny called Katie on his cell phone. He strode over to the lifeless body of Devin. His eyes open like a camera shutter.

"Katie, we got him. Get the police to come to the old Redwood Asylum," Kenny said. "On second thought, send everyone. We got some bodies in here."

"Are you okay?" she asked.

"A couple of stab wounds I can shake off. Oh, save me that vodka. I will need it," Kenny said in a sarcastic tone. "I'm happy to hear your voice."

Katie wiped the tears from her eyes and laughed. "I'll have that drink ready for you. Come home."

"Yes, ma'am!" Kenny said as he smiled.

"I am so glad you two are safe," Robert said trying to hold back tears.

"Dad, I---" Jordan said.

"I know son. I love you too."

Jordan pulled back. "Dad, I'm sorry for how I treated you."

"Actually, I'm the one who is sorry. I may have screwed up as a husband." Robert looked up at Amber. "But, I wanted to be the father that you could look up too and depend on. I want you to know, no matter what, that I'll always be there for you and Kevin."

"Thanks, Dad," Jordan said. "I just want to get out of here and see him and Jennifer."

"I understand let's all get out of here," Robert said.

"You look like shit," Amber said.

"Yeah, you should see the other guy," Robert said laughing while grimacing from his stab wound.

Amber noticed the blood on Robert's shirt.

"Hey, are you okay?"

"It's just a flesh wound."

She left up his shirt. "It is more than a flesh wound. You should see a doctor."

"I appreciate your concern and I will take you up on your wise counsel."

"Wow, wonders never cease! Robert Maxwell actually took my advice. Hell has really frozen over." She pulled off a playful smile.

"People can surprise you." Robert winked with one eye.

"Robert, I didn't get a chance to thank you for saving Jordan and me," Amber said. "If you weren't around, that monster would have got away with whatever he was planning." She paused trying to block her mind of the trauma endured by Devin.

"It's nothing Amber. All that matters is that you and Jordan are safe. That's all that matters. I know you and I had a rocky marriage in the past, but I would like to be a part of Jordan's and Kevin's life."

"Okay," she said.

"Great, I promise you. You won't regret this."

"But, there is one condition. Don't bring any of your girlfriends over when you visit."

"You got yourself a deal. On the record, I'm not seeing anyone. So you, Jordan, and Kenny can stop by the house."

"We shall see," Amber said.

They all exited the room passing through halls, the sound of sirens were heard from outside the facility. Casey and Sam stood in front of the asylum, staying close to each other. Relief was written on her face knowing that the police arrived.

"It's all over," Robert said with a smile walking toward the car with his friends in family.

* * *

On the next day, Robert was about to be discharged from the Redwood Hospital after twelve hours of observation. He devoured the remaining chocolate pudding, laying on the bed, watching the latest news headlines on the death of the Mannequin Killer. The idea that Devin was dead brought comfort to his heart. He turned up the volume on the TV monitor mounted on the wall, hearing the sordid details of the alleged serial killer.

A nurse with black curly hair and brown eyes wearing blue scrubs. She walked into the room to check on him. "How is our patient doing today?"

"For the first time in a while, I'm feeling great."

"That's good to hear."The nurse was checking on Robert's stomach bandages, lifting up his blue open gown. She glimpsed at the TV monitor, hearing about The Mannequin Killer."I can't believe that creep is dead. He caused so much pain in our community. It is nice to know that justice was served. I still think about all the families that this monster had destroyed."

"I know what you mean."

"I'm sorry, I tend to babble. The stitches seem to be holding up and there seems to be no bleeding from the bandages. You are cleared to go. You can sign the release form at the front desk when you are ready. Do you need anything else?"

"No, I am satisfied. You have been good to me Heather. Thank you."

A smile creased on her face. "Have a good day Mr. Maxwell." She walked out of the room.

There was a knock on the wall. Everyone showed up to check up on him. His son Jordan greeted him with a hug. On his right, Robert saw Jennifer, Kenny, Katie, Kevin, and Amber. From his left view, Toad and Zack. Robert decided to adopt Sam since he had no family who could care for him and was planning on getting the adoption papers filled out by the end of the week.

"Hey, Dad, how are you feeling?" Jordan asked.

"I'm feeling good, son. I am happy you all came," Robert said.

"Hi papa," Kevin said, hugging him.

"Hey, little man," Robert said. "I missed you."

"I miss you too, papa. I got something for you."

"What you got for me?" Robert said with curious eyes.

Kevin pulled up a green card from his small white bag with a red hand print inside. Robert saw a small smelly face signed by Jordan, Jennifer and Kevin.

"Thank you, Kevin I love this card," Robert kissed his forehead.

Jennifer walked to Robert.

"Thank you for saving Jordan and amber," Jennifer said.

"Oh, you don't have to thank me. We are practically family," Robert said.

"I'm sorry, for the way I treated you when we met at the police department. I was terrified. I should've said those things to you," Jennifer said.

"Hey, the only thing that mattered to me was Jordan and Amber's safety and that they are alive. All is forgiven."

"Hmm, I was wrong about you," Jennifer said. "You are a good man, Robert."

Robert smirked. "I'll take the compliment."

Jennifer took Kevin by the hand. Come on, Kevin let's see what we can get at the vending machine.

"Okay, bye papa!" Kevin said.

"Bye, Kevin," Robert said.

"And what? Miss out on the guy who took on two psychopaths in a signal night. I wouldn't check out on this for the world," Kenny said, reaching out for his hand. "Good to see you are in good health." He hugged him.

"Glad you stop by to crash the party," Robert said in a joking tone.

"Hey, Mr. Maxwell Zack and I got this for you," Toad said, giving him a black T-shirt that had the written inscription, on the front, Badass Cop.

"I love it thank you boys, I will be wearing this," Robert said.

"No, problem Mr. Maxwell. I hope you feel better. Come on, Zack we got to head over to the gaming store to pick up The First of Us part two."

"Zack, you drive safe out there,"Kenny said.

"Don't worry, Dad. I learn from the best," Zack said.

"They grow up so fast," Kenny said. "I never thought I would see in the hospital."

Robert laughed. "Me either."

"How is Sam?" Kenny asked.

"He is over at Virgil's. Safe and sound," Robert said.

"So, you really are gonna adopt him?"

"I can't see why not. It would be better than being in a foster home for him. You know how that system works."

"I get it. I forgot. I stopped by your house earlier and picked up your mail that you asked for. I find this package by the doorstep. It had no return address."

Robert examined a white envelope. He tore into it and felt the smooth texture of the bubble wrap inside feeling for an object. As his hand came up, everyone in the room noticed it was a black cell phone with a note written in red letters that reads play me. Robert removed the note and pushed on the play button on the video recording, revealing the image of Devin.

"Hello, Detective Maxwell. If you are getting this recording, then I'm most likely dead. I have something to tell you. A confession if you will. You remember David Swanson? The charming FBI agent. Well, it turns out he made a deal with me. He would supply me access to files and other resources of all the police involved in my father's murder an exchange for my brother's release from prison. That's right, you heard me, I have another twin. It took a lot of red tape, but it was worth it. You think I was bad, you haven't seen anything yet. See you in hell."

The recording ended. Robert gasped at the realization that Devin had another brother, a triplet. Panic and stress felt in the room. The eerie feeling that couldn't be flushed out.

"The game is not over," Robert said.

Somewhere outside the bus terminal was a man exiting the bus with his black luggage as he wheeled away, walking toward the transportation station. He looked at the display guide getting the layout of the place. The man noticed a young woman and her baby in a black stroller, sitting by the wooden bench. He marched in their direction.

"Excuse me, I don't mean to bother you. Do you know where I can find Terminal 3? I'm a little lost here," the man said.

"Yeah, you go right and then go left taking the escalator up. Then, you go straight until you reach the end and you will see Terminal 3."

"Thank you so much. "Did anyone tell you, you have nice eyes?" The man smiled revealing all his white teeth.

"Thanks, I appreciate it."

The man turned and walked away blending in with the crowd, whistling.

Ingram Content Group UK Ltd.
Milton Keynes UK
UKHW020042210623
423741UK00006B/56